Classic City Murders Vol. I-II

ISBN-13: 978-0-9972920-4-6
ISBN-10: 0-9972920-4-0

First printing, December, 2016

Cover design by ThomasMax

Front cover illustration courtesy of clipartpanda.com

Author's websites: www.13decisions.com
www.sheilahudsonwriter.com

Published by:

tm

ThomasMax Publishing
P.O. Box 250054
Atlanta, GA 30325
Website: thomasmax.com

Classic City Murders Vol. I-II

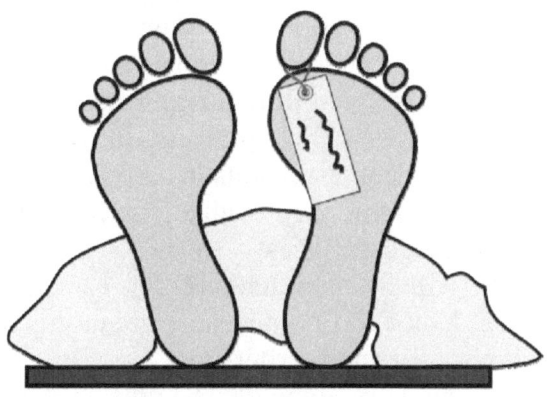

Sheila S. Hudson

ThomasMax

Your Publisher
For The 21st Century

A Word from the Publisher

You are reading a book that won the ThomasMax "You Are Published" annual contest at the Southeastern Writers Association's annual conference and workshop, an event held for four decades on beautiful St. Simons Island. Although Sheila, former President of SWA, has won many awards at the workshop, this is her first time to win our ThomasMax contest.

If you are a writer, I urge you to attend SWA's annual workshop and conference, offering instructors from many phases of the industry. SWA always has at least one, sometimes two, novel instructors, and often features classes on poetry, non-fiction (general or specific topics), writing inspirational works, writing for young readers, writing short fiction and a host of other topics. These topics and the instructors rotate annually. SWA also has an agent from a major literary agency to whom attendees can pitch or discuss their projects. In addition, SWA offers contests (the ThomasMax contest results in a book deal, but most of the contests have cash prizes) and *free* evaluations by instructors in up to three different manuscript categories.

The 2017 event will be held June 16-20. The host will again be Epworth-by-the-Sea. You can find out more about this annual event by visiting the website, southeasternwriters.org.

When we at ThomasMax judge contest entries, we have no idea of the author's identity. This insures fairness to all entrants. All other SWA contests are judged similarly to prevent any personal prejudice.

We hope to see you in 2017 or at one of our future annual events. It's the greatest "bang for the buck" writers' training you will ever receive. In a sequestered atmosphere in a resort setting, both experienced and beginning writers will find friends, contacts and, of course, instruction in ways that have led to success. It's all about *Writers Helping Writers.* Don't just take my word for it, though; do some research and you'll see that it's pretty much a universal sentiment from all those who attend that SWA offers the best instruction in writing across many different fields at a surprisingly affordable price. As former SWA President, and an instructor at the 2017 workshop, I am a bit biased, but success has come to many SWA participants, including current President Buzz Bernard.

--- Lee Clevenger, President, ThomasMax Publishing

This series is dedicated to my real partners in crime writing. The first is Ms. Amy Munnell, who tirelessly volunteers her time as my editor, confidante, and writing buddy. She is brilliant in her understanding of our target audience. She knows all my foibles, all my favorite pitfalls, and patiently herds me back on task with kindness and grace that I don't deserve. I am thrilled that she has taken on the task as my editor but most of all I value her as a friend.

My other partner in crime writing is my husband of 48 years, Tim Hudson. He has pushed, cajoled, and provided so that I could follow my dream to become an author. All that I have accomplished is because of his unselfishness and his belief in my abilities.

I love you both. - Sheila

Classic City Murders
Book I
Partners in Crime

1

The knife blade glittered in the afternoon sun; she closed her eyes and prayed. She'd heard that in the last moments, your life passed before your eyes. With blood pounding in her temples, Louisa opened her heavily lidded eyes and forced herself to stare into the face of the man who had raped her and murdered her mother!

"I'm home."

The back door slammed and reality kicked in. Quentin was home. It was always jarring when I had to switch gears, remove my alter ego, and become the little woman of the household.

Stella Holmes was not the name given to me at Crawford Long Hospital in Atlanta, but a moniker that I had chosen. Since I devoted much of my adolescent and teen years reading everything Arthur Conan Doyle had ever written, I made the last name of my nom de plume Holmes an homage to the great man. Stella means star and that's what I aim for -- a star writer of cozy mysteries. At the time I didn't think anyone would ever see what I had written. I never dreamed it would be the launch of a secret writing career.

It may have been my pen name that prompted me to write mysteries or maybe it was to collect on a bet from an old college roommate. In any case, once a publisher offered me a three-book deal the name stuck. I engaged an agent and the rest took off. My only doubt was: Could I manage to keep up the charade and shield my ultra-conservative husband from the truth?

I was told my books were good reads. They flew off the shelves even in a competitive market. My novels contained the formula that sold: discreet love scenes, action and adventure, plot-thickening twists by likeably flawed characters sprinkled with humor. The local book reviewer described my style as "Jan Karon meets Mary Higgins Clark" which pleased me to no end.

I closed my laptop and saved my latest manuscript on a USB which I plopped into my pocket. Quentin went into his study and then upstairs to change from his suit to more casual clothes. I often wished that I could share my success with the person I loved most, but I'm afraid my scribblings might embarrass him. I told myself that when the time was right I would reveal all including a chunk of my royalties in a local bank under Stella's name. What I was doing was for our retirement cottage in the mountains or on the seashore whichever he wanted.

"How was your day, dear?"

Quentin shook his head.

"Not good. The department chair wants to make radical cuts in the budget while the faculty is screaming for lab equipment, ergonomic desk chairs, and new computers. Same old. Same old. Let's not talk about it anymore, it gives me indigestion."

I nodded in agreement and plated roast beef, mashed potatoes, and gravy. I could hear our veins clotting with cholesterol. Fortunately, I didn't serve this very often.

"What did you do today?" he asked helping himself to biscuits and more gravy.

"Oh, nothing unusual. Went to Barnes and Nobel, browsed, and had a quick lunch downtown."

I knew he wasn't listening closely so I was careful not to be too specific. I suspect he skipped lunch by the portions on his plate. A long walk after dinner would help both our stress levels and health concerns.

In real life, I am Stephanie Hart, wife to Professor Hart of Rutherford Community College. We enjoy our little corner of the world nestled in the heart of northeast Georgia. Quentin teaches English and Comparative Literature but he has specialties in cults and the occult. We met in graduate school and have been married more than 30 years. For a short time I taught a few classes, but now I play housewife and write.

For as long as I can remember, I have wanted to write. My head is full of stories but growing up I was reluctant to write them down because my mother warned that men do not want girls who were smarter than they are. I quickly learned that was mostly true so I didn't date much until my college days. I filled numerous journals and diaries with ideas that my 'little gray cells' provided in the way of story material plus scandals only available in a community not even large enough to be a "hick" town. I devoured every mystery that Agatha Christie and Arthur Conan Doyle cranked out.

"How about that walk now?" I asked after mentally reworking the last chapter.

"Good idea. I need your perspective on some of the items we discussed during the faculty meeting."

We grabbed jackets to fend off the evening breeze and exited the front door. No need to lock up. Nothing ever happened here. This was the most honest town in the world.

Life here was far from challenging. I suppose that's what charged my writing battery. When we married I imagined a quiet academic lifestyle with 2.5 children, a house with a picket fence, a wood-paneled station wagon and a cocker spaniel. There we would live happily ever after.

Some of that came true. Quentin was good at his job, maybe too good.

"Dr. Mills wants me to take the offer of becoming a part-time consultant with the police department. The package comes with a salary supplement. That will help us personally and the positive public relations will be good for the college. With my research and background on occult studies, the chief feels that I could be of great use to them. Dr. Mills has already announced that there will be no cost of living raises this year and this means . . ."

". . this means the police furnish your pay raise and the university gets free publicity" I interrupted.

"That's about it," he laughed and took my hand.

We turned the corner. Living here was convenient. We could walk downtown – if you could call a drug store, bank, newspaper office, and a five-and-dime downtown. The church was within walking distance and so was the grocery if you only needed a couple of items.

The Golden Agers met at the Pancake House next to the grocery. It was from my time with the senior citizens, especially Doris and Carol, that I got the idea for my first diva book. They took me into their confidences and taught me how to cheat at cards, talk like a pirate, and in general have serious fun.

Whatever it was, the synapses started firing again. With my silver haired buddies, I got the low down on the weekly Bible study, the annual church bazaar, and the monthly ladies' social and service society. I learned how to embellish and exaggerate. I began to write down some of this stuff, mix in a few 'who dun its' for my own amusement, and on a whim I sent a manuscript into a publisher and voila a career was born.

"Hey what planet are you on?" Quentin asked.

"Sorry. I've got a lot of things on my mind right now. What were you saying?"

"Ice cream. Do you want some?"

"Yes, sweetie of course," I answered somewhat chagrinned that my husband caught me in a world filled with protagonists, antagonists, and wondering how I could write Louisa away from her attacker. I imagined a few plot points to get my heroine out of a tight spot, but I wasn't pleased with any of them. Before he came home, I managed to jot down a few possibilities on the USB in my pocket. I'd run them by Carol and Doris. They had become my first readers and biggest fans. Of course, they were sworn to secrecy, a bargain they had kept for three years.

Who knew that my very first book, *The Diva Code*, would be so popular? So far I managed to keep personal information off the book jackets and out of the news. I worked hard to keep my worlds separated. When I wasn't involved with the seniors, writing, or accompanying Quentin to university functions, I volunteered for various community functions. My double life was perfect. By day, I was ordinary but by night, I wrote of murder, crime, adventure, life, and love in a small town.

2

Labor Day, my favorite weekend of the year, was fast approaching. The entire town pitched in to help with the City Wide Barbecue. Our whole community came together for the grand event.

Traditionally the men stayed up all Friday night cooking Boston butt pork shoulders in City Park and listening to Bluegrass music. From what I could tell, they spun a few yarns of their own. Oh to be able to record some of them!

Saturday was the big dinner where barbecue sauce flowed like wine. The women provided the cakes and pies for dessert along with cole slaw, bread, and pickles. Every year the City Wide Barbecue was a huge success with the proceeds going to the local homeless shelters.

This year Quentin was commissioned with preparing the meat using his secret sauce. With my hubby's mind occupied, it was easy to make quick work of dinner tomorrow night and send him off to gather ingredients.

I rinsed and placed the dishes in the dishwasher. I stretched out in my leather chair with a glass of wine to watch the 10 p.m. news. It was exhausting to envision every kitchen in town bustling with preparations for Saturday. There would be events for children including relays, races, eating contests, and the coup de gras – the parade. For our burg, it was bigger than the Fourth of July.

I thought over my conversation about Quentin being a consultant for the police department. He had worked with the local authorities on several crimes involving the occult. But this last offer was a more lucrative partnership at least from what I understood. Since aiding in the Matamoras murders, Quentin had become a hot commodity. He taught summer courses at the college in symbology, the occult, and cultic sects. Each time he taught the seminar, the classes grew. Either it was his superb instruction or the interest was growing. In either case, I was proud of my husband who was the genius behind bringing a number of criminals to justice.

On the other hand, I reserved concern for his well-being. In the back of my mind I feared retribution from those who were prosecuted. The media freely listed his name and occupation as part of the breaking stories, but the police chief assured me of their protection.

I sipped my Chardonnay and smiled with pride. We were very happy doing what we loved. I didn't mind that my fame was a secret.

When the time was right I would reveal my nom de plume. I knew that Quentin would be happy for me. I just wanted his career to be priority.

As for me, I had big plans for Stella. If my novels remain successful, I planned to purchase a retirement cottage with the royalties. Quentin needed a relaxing hobby when he wasn't teaching or being a consultant. Fishing seemed a great option. And as a writer, I could perform my tasks anywhere there was an internet connection.

3

Every man in town who was between diapers and Depends© was at City Park helping with the barbecue. Quentin left class early on Friday and went straight to the park, so I didn't even need to make dinner. He had stashed everything he needed in the car before class. I knew he was in his element once he donned his apron and began preparations for the secret pork rub and barbeque sauce.

Quentin returned home around 2 a.m. and slept for a few hours but was up and gone before breakfast. I slept late and ate a small breakfast. I wanted to leave room for the spread at noon. I finished cleaning up in the kitchen and heard a car in the driveway. I assumed Quentin had forgotten something. I went to open the front door, but no one was there. 'Someone must have turned around' I told myself.

By the time I got to City Park with my contribution to the BBQ, the crowd was checking in for their barbecue plates. I helped distribute the food and we watched the parade. Quentin went home exhausted. I stayed behind since I was part of the BBQ clean-up crew.

The entire time we were cleaning my editor's voice boomed through my head: 'You've got to have a little more sexual tension.' Now how was I to manage that? I had to think of my readership. What if my family read my books? What if the faculty at the college where Quentin taught was a fan of my novels?

Still I had to give the editor and the public what they wanted, keep it entertaining but at the same time wholesome and above all tell a good story. That is a tall order for any writer. I went to bed with all of this on my mind and dreamed of an old boyfriend, a baby out of wedlock, and a murder. But wait. Who said anything about murder?

4

I awoke with a start. Someone was banging at our glass sliding doors. Police cars and sirens with swirling red and blue lights lit up our driveway. Astronauts could locate our house from the moon. My phone began to ring. I ignored it and opened the door to an insistent detective who asked a lot of questions. I put up my hand and tried to remain calm.

"Wait a second. I need coffee," I said to the officer who flashed credentials at me.

"What's going on?" Quentin asked as he stumbled into the kitchen. After the barbeque we were both exhausted but managed to talk into the night about what this business of being part-time as a police consultant meant – both to his career and to our personal life.

While we waited on the slowest Mr. Coffee in the world, the detective, now identified as Sgt. Grimes, explained that a dead body was discovered in the car parked in front of our house. The victim was a man. The deceased still had his credit cards and wallet so robbery as a motive was ruled out. Edmund Tolbert, as the identification revealed, apparently died by asphyxiation. It seems the old Pontiac emitted carbon monoxide fumes. The driver must have fallen asleep while it was idling. But why was he parked in front of our house? The name Tolbert didn't ring a bell, yet here he is dead practically on our doorstep.

The sergeant asked us a slew of questions about our activities while his team began a search of the house and grounds. A uniform presented the Sarge with a bulging file folder that he found underneath our king size bed.

"What's this?" Grimes asked as he plopped the folder in front of me. It was the galleys for my latest novel, *Diva's Revenge*, about a murderer who gets even with an old boyfriend after being jilted.

"It's mine," I admitted. Quentin's eyebrows went up but he played it cool.

"But the title page says it was written by Stella Holmes."

"I know. I'm Stella Holmes," I said averting my husband's glances. I took a large gulp of coffee and explained about the nom de plume and my writing career.

The detective shook his head. "I'm sorry but I'm going to have to take this for now."

"I don't see why. It has nothing to do with this homicide."

"Really. Did I mention that the victim died while holding a book autographed by Stella Holmes?"

Quentin gave me a look that I'd never seen before. He couldn't believe that a bestselling author, namely me, had kept this secret from him. I feared that he would be angry at my secretiveness. If he was angry, he didn't show it publicly instead he pushed out his chest and almost crowed.

"Why didn't you tell me?" Quentin asked when we were finally alone.

"At first, it was just a hobby. When the first one got published, it was a fluke. Then things took off and it seemed better to leave things as they were. Are you mad?"

"Mad? No but I'm a little hurt but all in all I'm ecstatic. And so proud I could burst. But the good detective said that the victim had a book of yours in his hand. So do you know him?"

"Not by the name Edmund Tolbert. But anyone could buy that book either at the bookstore or on line. That doesn't mean anything."

"But it was signed, so you had to have met him somewhere."

"That's true," I mused.

"Do you think he was trying to contact you?" my husband asked.

"I suppose. I am so sorry that you had to find out this way, but truthfully I am relieved that you know. I don't like keeping secrets. More coffee?"

We talked for hours after the police left. I told him the details of the last three years regarding my writing profession. The only book signings I had done were at least two hours away. I hadn't let them post a photograph or give any details as to our address so how did this fellow find me?

As they normally do in small towns, rumors flew. Was Stephanie Hart, wife of the local professor, a best-selling novelist? The congregation where we worshipped held an emergency meeting. So did the college where Quentin taught. Our conservative southern berg had definite ideas about the "woman who wrote trashy novels."

Doris and Carol were excited that I was in their words, ***famous***. But best of all they were credited as my inspiration. A few of our acquaintances held their opinions to themselves. The few who withdrew from us were the usual snobs. As usual the 'bodice ripper' accusations were raised by the ones who hadn't bothered to read *The*

Diva Code, *Southern Diva*, or *Divine Diva*.

Quentin used his oratory expertise to quiet the misgivings of his colleagues. He encouraged everyone to take the long view and reserve judgment. Besides there was something more important at stake than who wrote what – namely a death that had occurred in front of a professor's home. Was it a coincidence that the same professor was also a police consultant? Quentin was wonderful at debate and now showing his vulnerabilities. But I noticed in every spare moment, he devoured all of my books so that he could more properly defend my writing prowess.

The autopsy came back on the dead reverend or pseudo-reverend. He was indeed none other than an old acquaintance of mine. The deceased, Edmund Tolbert, was in reality Ed Lawson. We attended the same college and even worked on a few projects together years ago. Media was touting him as an "old flame" which was a stretch. Ed had changed his name and recently moved to our community under the guise of joining the staff of the local Catholic church.

Quentin had a lot of questions about this guy. I explained that from what I could remember Ed had always been socially dysfunctional. But that didn't explain the name change unless he decided to make a clean breast of his old life. But more importantly, why was he parked in front of my house holding a copy of the *Diva Code* in his cold dead hands?

Sgt. Grimes confirmed my credentials with the editor at Avalon. The local authorities couldn't wait to release their findings to the press telling the whole world that Stella Holmes was really Stephanie Hart. Local media had already "leaked" most of the details anyway including a college photo of me with the deceased at a Christmas formal. I wonder where they dug that up. The reporter also listed details about Quentin complete with his activities as professor turned police consultant. Quentin was not exactly thrilled with the spotlight.

And there was more. I hadn't exactly told the police everything. About a year ago, my editor thought it would be a good research opportunity to visit Chatoog Center, a minimum security facility for white collar crime. My next *Diva* book had a character who went to jail for fraudulent tax reports. Pamela Ford, my agent, suggested that the experience would enrich the sequel. I researched some of the facts, toured the center, did a book signing, and there he was – Ed Lawson, a face from the past. We chatted about old times and that was that. That's when he got the autographed book! That had been at least a year ago.

Ed was incarcerated in connection with a financial fraud. He swore he was innocent and vowed that when he got out he would prove it. I wonder if impersonating a priest was part of that plan.

About a month after the book signing, Ed's letters started coming via the publisher. I only opened the first one. He sounded too passionate about our history, so I stuffed his other letters into a bureau drawer underneath lingerie. Then as suddenly as the letters came, they stopped. Since no one knew anything about Stella Holmes, the novels, or the book signing gigs, I forgot all about it.

I wonder how much of this I should confess and how much I should keep to myself. If Ed died of asphyxiation then I didn't want to stir the pot with accusations. But what if there was foul play. . .?

5

November arrived and brought autumn leaves, barbecues, and elections. Fortunately elections moved our notoriety to the back burner. That was old news. And that's what Stella Holmes was now – old news. The ruffled feathers smoothed eventually. Edmund Tolbert aka Ed Lawson's death was ruled a suicide, which I didn't believe. Whether or not he was a 'man of the cloth' was another issue. A friend worked at the coroner's office and got me a copy of the report.

Asphyxiation was listed as cause of death. From the report he had all the classic symptoms even blue lips. From the little I knew about poisons, I recalled that some varieties can mimic asphyxiation and impersonate carbon monoxide. The description said that Ed wore typical priest clothes and had an old picture of me crumpled in his suit coat. So that's where the press got that picture.

Back home to my Agatha Christie books, the PDR, and the internet for more research. Ed would probably be amused if I gave him a starring role in my next novel. And that reminds me, the good sergeant hadn't returned my galleys. I had to give them one more edit before I mailed them back to my editor. He wanted them as soon as he returned from his Caribbean cruise. If I sold enough copies of *Diva's Revenge* perhaps Quentin and I could afford a cruise.

It was time to give the good sergeant a call or perhaps a visit.

6

Larry Alewine was running for mayor against the incumbent. The Alewine slogan is *Family – First and Foremost*. The Alewines are a prominent family in our burg. Larry's wife, Beth, and I were friends at one point in our lives, but Beth's career aspirations trumped everything. The Alewine dynasty was all about blue bloods, aristocracy, and breeding. It marked everything the family touched. No scandal has ever been linked to them, no skeletons in the closet, and no out of wedlock surprises, indiscretions, or quickie annulments. Like a mini-Mafia they had done their job well. Squeaky clean and honest as the day is long at least according to the local newspaper. I suspect if you dug back far enough there was an Alewine ancestor in the editor's chair.

Beth's aspirations had always controlled her life but accelerated after law school. She clerked in the law offices of Benton and Motley rising through the ranks until she caught the eye of Larry Alewine. Beth joined their staff in 1990 and joined their family in 1993. Only taking time out for Larry, Jr. in 1995, Beth climbed her way to the top and was now a junior partner in the firm. Indeed, Beth had it all and she wasn't about to lose it. Just how far she would go to protect her holdings was to be tested.

As luck or politics would have it. Beth's husband, Larry, was the current Chair of the Personnel Committee at the Episcopalian Church. Larry had interviewed the deceased, Ed Lawson aka Fr. Edmund Tolbert for a staff position. This made Larry possibly the last person to see Ed Lawson alive. During the interview Edmund confessed that he was an ex-offender and wanted a second chance. He produced evidence that he had changed his ways and was studying for the priesthood.

When Larry decided not to recommend Ed to the personnel committee, he took umbrage and lashed out according to the statements Larry made to the police. The secretary at the Episcopal Church overheard Ed make threats that the Alewines would be sorry for the way he was treated. The shouting was obvious and there were a lot of witnesses to this outburst. This begged the question: Was Ed blackmailing someone? Is that what got him killed? Was it a coincidence that he was in the same town as me with my book and my picture? I didn't think the police would buy that story. So I decided to visit Beth in her law office. Maybe Larry told her something he hadn't shared with the police.

"Beth, did you know Ed before he came to town?" I asked.

"Absolutely not. I don't know why he applied for that job at the church. Larry said he wasn't qualified at all and was more interested in spouting his ridiculous theories. Obviously, the man had mental problems. I don't know anything about this ancient story in some newspaper either," she flung the article at me.

I scanned the article and remembered it like yesterday. It was coverage of the slaughter of a newborn the University of Georgia fifteen years ago. No one was ever charged in the murder. The case was cold with no clues and no suspects. Just a butchered infant laid to rest without a name on a cold day in January.

"I was a graduate student when this happened. It rocked my world," I confessed. I looked up from the article to see Beth wipe away a tear with a tissue.

"Mine too," she whispered and turned toward the window.

While her back was turned, I pocketed the tissue in hopes of finding some answers.

"Oh, Beth. I am sorry to be so insensitive. It forgot that it was during this same time that your sister. . . um . . . disappeared. This stirs up painful memories, I'm sure. So what was Ed's theory that involved you?" I asked.

"I don't have a clue, but when he produced this article, Larry threw him out on his ear. I was nowhere near the Athens campus when this occurred. I had an internship with a firm in Augusta that entire semester. I, like the rest of the world, only knew what the media revealed. Of course it was a heartbreaking event.

"When I did come home a few days after this story broke, my mother revealed that Lilith left school and she didn't know where she was. I've since had no contact and presume she is dead.

"Mr. Lawson's visit was quite upsetting to Larry and to me. One thing Larry said Ed kept repeating was that he was coming back," Beth said.

"What do you think he meant by saying that?" I asked.

Beth regained her poise, but she had shown me the chink in her armor. She sat back down at her desk and the hard shelled Alewine was back.

"I've told the police just what I told you. This Ed person was crazed and obviously desperate. I don't know any more than I've told everyone. I don't want to be rude but please leave."

I thought about our conversation as I turned the corner at Hamilton Avenue and Haight Street. Obviously Ed's visit to the Alewines had touched a nerve. How much of Beth's past did Larry know? Was she hiding the history about her sister? What if anything did it have to do with the news article?

The car automatically turned into the driveway of my childhood home. I often come here to think things out. Sometimes I bring my laptop and work out the plots of my books, draw character sketches, or research background for my novels. Today I just wanted solace and perhaps some clarity as to what was really going on.

The English Tudor stood like the monarch she was anchoring the dead end street. Her front porch and the old creaky wooden swing hung silently waiting. I spent the bulk of my girlhood here in this place. It remained gallantly, a little older and needing a paint job but as elegant as ever.

Thankfully, no neighbors were within sight so I stood on the porch for a few minutes basking in memories of reverent silence. The balcony, devoid of Mother's hanging plants and sun chairs, was bare except for the sense of a powerful presence, which lingered. The lawn now lay unkempt, the garden overrun with thorns and thistles like undisciplined, riotous children. The grass crept over the walkway. The flower garden lay still and silent, another victim of neglect. When my key turned in the lock, a chill ran through my soul. Am I unleashing the past or coming to grips with the present? What exactly did I hope to find here?

I took a quick turn of the first floor. Everything was in order. Quentin and I should put this house on the market, but doing so would be like selling part of my soul. Anyway the real estate market wasn't good so I got a temporary reprieve.

I sat my purse in the front room rocker and returned to the veranda. I sat in the swing for a while. It creaked with "porch music" just as I remembered. I needed that rhythm to collect and organize my thoughts.

My order of events included retrieving my book galleys from the police, find out what Ed said to Larry Alewine, unseal and read the rest of Ed's letters, and somehow make these puzzle pieces fit. But first I had a funeral to attend.

7

More out of curiosity than anything else, I attended the late Ed Lawson's memorial service. No relatives came to collect the body so it was purely a state sponsored event. Dr. Spencer was the minister on call. He briefed himself on what little the police furnished about the deceased's background. I had sympathy for his situation, but he did as well as anyone could under the circumstances.

I arrived as the organist completed the last strains of Amazing Grace so I slipped in and sat in the back row scanning those who attended. There were officials from the funeral home present to attend to details. No familiar faces that I could spot.

But wait. Beth Alewine was in attendance. Odd! She claimed that she didn't know Ed. Indeed she claimed she had never met him or even heard of him until the interview with Larry. Nevertheless, there she is in the darkest corner. Did Beth lie to me and to the police? Maybe she did know more than she let on. I left early before Beth could spot me. I had a friend in the police department and it was time to call in a favor.

* * *

"I could get in deep do-do for this Stephanie," Natalie reminded me as she pulled a banker's storage box from the shelf.

"Is it for one of your mysteries?" she continued.

"Uh, yes. Perhaps. I'm curious about who this guy really is and why he turned up in our town. I am supposed to know him but I really don't," I answered.

Natalie was nervous about bring the box out of the evidence room, but she sat it on the nearby table and reminded me, "Ten minutes and I have to get this back to the evidence room." I nodded.

"Thanks I owe you."

The doors closed behind Natalie and I was left to investigate the person behind this charade. I lifted out the contents: black trousers, black shirt, a crucifix, black shoes and socks, imitation leather wallet with a few dollars in it, and keys. A key to the car and another one, presumably to his lodgings. There was the crumpled photo of me and Ed at some school event. And last but not least Ed's copy of *The Diva*

Code.

My hands trembled as I opened the flyleaf and there was my signature: *Thanks, Stella Holmes.* It took me a moment to remember that day when I signed books at the Chatoog Center. Ed was friendly enough. We chatted a little and I moved on to the next person in line. Then he said something peculiar as I left. What was it now? It was a quote that I thought odd at the time but now it made more sense.

There are no secrets that time does not reveal.

What secrets? How will they be revealed? I slipped the copy of *The Diva Code* into my pocket, replaced the lid on the evidence box, and texted Natalie that I was through. Evidence gets lost or misplaced all the time. I had to trust the authorities wouldn't discover it was missing until I could replace it.

At home I began methodically going through the book I swiped from the police. Nothing was obvious for the first fifty pages. Then on page 51 I struck gold: "dimly lit rooms encourage dangerous crimes." I made a sandwich and searched on through chapter after chapter jotting down highlighted words and notes scribbled in the margins. I also googled the quote that Ed mentioned that day at Chatoog. It was from Jean Racine whose life was a tragedy in itself.

Could I prove that this was Ed's handwriting? And would I be able to put together some kind of time line for these jottings?

I was interrupted as Quentin came home from dinner. It wasn't quite time to let him in on this so I placed my day's sleuthing in a drawer. We had the usual evening conversation. Afterwards, Quentin went upstairs to read. I cleaned up the kitchen and only pulled out the book and my notes when I knew my husband was fast asleep.

At 2 a.m. I awoke at my desk with my notes sprawled out everywhere. I had gone through most of *The Diva Code* and accumulated a lot of words and phrases. Ed had devised a code of his own. He must have anticipated some kind of foul play to go to all this trouble. It must have been some sort of insurance. I was too tired to make sense of it. Maybe Quentin or my favorite curmudgeonly uncle could help.

8

"Hi Uncle Harry," I called out.

"Hello yourself," he answered. "I'm on the back porch. Come on out."

I used my key to unlock the front door, tossed my overstuffed tote onto the couch, and grabbed a cup of coffee on my way out to the greenhouse. No matter the weather, my favorite uncle could always be counted on to have everything wide open.

Uncle Harry aka Colonel Harry Roberts, U.S. Army Retired, was not really my uncle but a close friend of the family. I assumed that he had heard the news about my alter ego and would read me the riot act about keeping secrets. Instead, he was poised over a plant tenderly clipping off dead leaves and inspecting its health.

"What'cha doing?"

"Trying to bring this castor plant back to health," he answered.

"Another poisonous addition to your little shop of horrors?" I asked.

"But of course. I study them for their healing properties as well as for their deadly ones."

Harry smiled and put away his looking glass and tiny clippers. I loved this strange little man who had been my surrogate father for many years. I used what he had taught me about poisons in much of my research. Although I never really announced that I wrote novels I always suspected that he knew.

Everyone is not privileged to have medical knowledge like Agatha Christie so an author uses what she has. Harry was my ace in the hole when it came to knowledge of all things deadly. He was a mystery novelist best friend.

"Have you been keeping up with the latest about the dead man in our driveway and the notorious person I've become?"

"Oh yes. But it's no surprise to me. I guessed long ago that you were more than met the eye. I've read most of Stella Holmes' books and a lot of the sample excerpts. I recognized the poisons and you even quoted me from time to time. Your father would be proud," he said.

"You think?"

"Absolutely. He spoke of you all the time when we were in business together and always with pride."

"And since you now know my secret and you are my favorite avuncular," I tried to flirt and laughed instead.

"And what would that be?" Harry answered.

"I need to know what would turn lips blue and kill you but may not necessarily be carbon monoxide poisoning."

"So you don't believe the police report?"

"No. I believe Ed Lawson was murdered because he was going to reveal something that would bring down an influential person. I think his clumsy attempt at blackmail got him killed. He died with my book in his hand, so maybe he was trying to tell me something. Anyway that's my crazy notion, so will you help me?"

"Sure. I'd be delighted," his eyes twinkled.

With his poison botanicals I believe that my uncle could come up with a variety of answers to my question. I would bet anything that if Ed Lawson was poisoned, as I posited, Uncle Harry would be just the person to find out how, with what, and when.

"I just need some time, the coroner's report, and any other details you can manage," Harry stated.

"Are you sure you aren't former CIA, FBI, KGB, or maybe MI6?" I asked trying to keep from smiling.

"Yes I'm sure. This is just a hobby, but you would be surprised how many people are interested in poisons, especially natural ones," he answered.

"I'm sure, but just know that I'm your number one fan," I responded. "How much time do you need?"

"I know where you live and also got your number, Stephanie or should I say Stella? I'll be in touch. But I'm serious, you must be careful. Someone has gone to a lot of trouble to get rid of Ed Lawson and cover up it up to look like an accident," he answered and did I detect a fatherly tone?

"Okay. I'll be careful. Here's a copy of the coroner's report, a list of words and phrases that Ed marked in *The Diva Code*, plus notes about the Alewines, and all I can remember about the last time I saw Ed at Chatoog Center where he was serving time for some fraud charge. And Uncle Harry, there's one more thing."

"Yes," Uncle Harry looked into my eyes.

"This is embarrassing. Quentin doesn't know, but Ed wrote me some letters. I made copies. I haven't even read them all myself. Would you mind?" I was humiliated but it had to be done.

"My dear, don't you know that I am totally at your service?" Harry squeezed my hand and said, "Besides, I always wanted to get something on the Alewine clan. Albert, that summa'bitch cheats at cards and stole my girlfriend in eleventh grade," Harry mumbled.

"Well I don't really don't believe Albert's involved since he's about ninety years old, but his son, Larry, and possibly his wife, Beth. Go on now and get to work." I feigned cracking a whip, laughed, gathered my things and left.

Harry blew me a kiss and returned to his poisonous darlings. His greenhouse held enough toxins to poison the state and maybe even the south. But I knew from our past discussions, that the same species that could kill could also be an ingredient for healing. It depended on the dosage.

9

Quentin went with me to the police station to retrieve my galleys for *Diva's Revenge*. Sgt. Grimes had conveniently 'forgotten' to return them. Fortunately I had other copies. I played devil's advocate with myself as to whether to let Quentin and the detective in on what had transpired in Beth Alewine's office. I relented and told Quentin most of it, but neither of them knew she was at Ed Lawson's funeral. But then they didn't know that I attended either. And of course, mum's the word about Uncle Harry's involvement.

"Here we are," Sgt. Grimes said as he plopped down my overstuffed folder.

"Just sign here that you are taking possession and it's off you go," he said. I could swear that he smiled. He didn't hide the fact that he was glad to be shed of me and my crazy theories. As far as the authorities were concerned, Ed Lawson died of asphyxiation from a faulty ventilation system in a late model Buick.

On our way home, Quentin popped the question.

"How would you respond to me taking a writing retreat for a few days?"

"I don't know. Okay I guess. Why? Do you think that this is a good time to be leaving town? I mean with the publicity and everything," I asked.

"It's impossible to finish my promotional dossier with all of this craziness about Ed, the upcoming election, your recent notoriety and all. I thought a few days of peace and quiet would be just the ticket. Doesn't Harry have a cabin a couple of hours away that we could use? That way it won't be too far or very expensive. What do you think?"

"When would you go? Couldn't you wait until after I publish *Diva's Revenge* and I could go with you?"

"I'm thinking I need the time now so I can get my dossier in order and finish the article for the Georgia Review. I've promised them an outline and a synopsis by January 1."

Quentin pulled into the driveway of our colonial. He switched off the ignition and pulled me close.

"I suppose you had better call Harry and make plans. I'll sure miss you though," I said.

"I know but it will only be a few days. Already things are calming down and people forget headlines pretty quickly. When the next big thing hits the media, we'll be old news and no one will even remember this."

Quentin said this with all sincerity, but by the next day his words came true. Because the next big thing was us.

10

"Yes this is Stephanie . . . Stella," I said over the phone. It was my agent. She was so excited that she was panting.

"Pamela, slow down. I can't understand a word you are saying."

She did slow down and it made me regret answering the telephone call. My first novel, *The Diva Code,* and the subsequent sequels were getting a lot of more attention since the death of Mr. Lawson.

Pamela has pitched my cozy as an ex-boyfriend reappears after many years and dies with my book clutched in his hand. She has gotten to some big wigs and got the powers that be in Hollywood to buy it. Those that rule the movie industry were supposedly sending some reps to follow up. Pamela Jones, my book agent, was about to have apoplexy before she could get out all of the details.

I was thrilled, scared, overjoyed, and fearful all at once. Pamela was on her way to our burg and she prayed that the paparazzi would follow. This was not what I bargained for. I had to reach Quentin and warn him that our quiet little village would soon be bustling.

His response was not what I expected.

"Who would you choose to play me? Ryan Gosling? George Clooney? No he's too old. What about Gerard Butler? I've always liked him."

"Quentin. Please get a hold of yourself. We don't even know if the movie people will be interested in my books. And if by some miracle, they buy the movie rights, it could be years and years before anything happens. There's been no offer. All of this is rumor and conjecture, Pamela has her head in the clouds and we've got bigger issues – like what about the fact that Ed may very well have been murdered?"

My voice tone kept getting higher and higher until I caught myself. Quentin gave me a startled look, took a sip of water, and went back to grading papers. After my little tirade, I went into the kitchen to start dinner but I could swear I heard mumbling. . . something about the actor who played Captain America.

"Of course this means I can't go to the cabin. What if they need me? After all I am a police consultant and considered an expert in many fields," Quentin said to no one in particular.

The next morning as I went to see Uncle Harry I couldn't believe the transformation. Shops had posted signs advertising my books. City workers were hanging banners with my picture. Doris and Carol flagged me down in front of the pharmacy. Luckily there was a parking space so I pulled in to see what all the hubbub was about.

"Hey girls," I called and rolled down the driver's side window.

"Isn't it exciting?" Doris called out. Carol nodded and beamed at me.

"Isn't what exciting?" I asked and was sure I would be sorry that I did.

"The movie. Hollywood. All of it," Doris continued her high-pitched tone.

"I don't know what you are talking about, ladies," although there was only one lady talking.

"We met your agent, Pamela, in the café. She told us all about the book deal, the movie rights, and all about auditions. I told her that Carol and I were your inspiration for the original diva book. Didn't I Carol? She said she might get us a bit part in the movie," Doris said.

Carol poised her lips to say something but instead just nodded an affirmation to what Doris already said.

"Pamela is here already?" I asked.

"Yes. Did I tell you that she said that once the writers and film crew got here they would begin casting for parts," Doris said with great authority.

"Jiminy Christmas, this is a zoo. I am the last to find out and I'm the author. I've got to find Pamela and put the kibosh on this madness," I said.

"I don't know why. The town is so enthusiastic. It's been quite a morale lifter. Every store has up signs and banners. The Barnes & Noble has a life size picture of you and the mall advertised that you were doing a book signing. I think it's lovely," Doris said.

"Lovely," Carol echoed.

I scratched my head, rolled up the window and wondered who engineered all this, when, and what was I going to do about it?

11

As I would have predicted Uncle Harry was in his greenhouse tinkering with his toxic trees and venomous vines. I prayed that the authorities would never get wind of his little greenhouse of death. And I am certainly not the one to inform on my greatest ally and source of all poisonous knowledge. In spite of the fact that I was afraid to touch anything in the entire greenhouse for fear of killing myself.

"Harry, where are you?" I called out as I came in the front door.

"I'm trimming the Choke Cherry and Lily-of-the-Valley plants," he answered.

I chucked my tote on the sofa and went straight back.

"I didn't know that Lily-of-the-Valley was poisonous," I said.

"Oh yes many of our favorite flowers are poisonous if ingested. All parts of the Lily-of-the-Valley are toxic including the red berries which may be attractive to children. If consumed even in small amounts, it can cause abdominal pain, vomiting, reduced heart rate, blurred vision, drowsiness, and red skin rashes.

"Other poisonous blooms are buttercups, Christmas Rose, Poinsettia, Snow-on-the-Mountain, and the Morning Glory, just to name a few."

"Wow. Everywhere you turn there are things that can kill you. So it's not only obvious things like rattlesnakes, cyanide, and toadstools," I gasped.

"Right you are. In the kitchen and bathroom are many items that are poisonous if misused. And of course, there's the local pharmacy with stocked with shelves of toxins. And if that's not enough you can shop for your poison at the local hardware, liquor, or grocery store," Harry added.

"That's not very cheery," I said. "Or helpful. I need to know what can cause someone to look like they've been asphyxiated but indeed died of something entirely different."

Just then my eye caught a corner of the room full of radiant lacy blossoms. I gravitated in that direction with my hand out to touch those beauties.

"Oooh those are pretty," I said.

Harry swatted my hand away.

"And deadly," he added. "I wear gloves for those babies. The hemlock and oleander are deadly from the root to the blossom. So deadly that if quail eat the seeds, which they are immune to, and you eat the quail flesh, you would either be paralyzed or die from the results."

I snapped back my hand and paid attention to what Harry was saying.

"I have narrowed down the symptoms to methanol which is distilled from fermented grain and commonly found in moonshine. If Mr. Lawson did imbibe in this homemade liquor, his body would have metabolized it as formaldehyde. That is assuming he didn't drink antifreeze, perfume, paint remover or varnish; methanol is in those as well. It would have taken from twelve to twenty-four hours for the headache, pain, shallow respiration, cyanosis, and finally death to occur. By that time you would be hard pressed to find any residue in the body. If methane is the culprit that killed your mystery man, where would he get moonshine in our peaceful little community?"

"I think I might know where," I said. I hugged Uncle Harry. We closed up the greenhouse and were going into the parlor when the doorbell rang.

Harry answered the door and Pamela poured herself into our presence. I made the introductions and Harry offered coffee. I declined for both of us, made an excuse that we had to have a discussion, and walked Pamela out of the door. No way was she going to muscle in on my private line to Poisons Are Us.

"Your uncle is handsome, that is for a man of his maturity," Pamela gushed.

"Yes, Harry is a sweetheart. But how did you find me?"

"Simple. I asked Quentin and he gave me your uncle's address," she said. "Quentin is as excited over the movie proposition as I am."

"Yes I know he is in a quandary over what actor will play him. And we don't even have confirmation that there will be a movie," I said.

Pamela had a strange look in her eye.

"Pamela Jones. What have you done?"

"Actually, the people with Lion Gate Entertainment and I had a very short, informal sit down this morning at the local café," she answered.

"Wonderful. That's like making an announcement with a bullhorn. Everyone in town already knows more than I do. Do you realize a man died because of something he connected with someone in this town, my book, and possibly a newspaper article? What's wrong with everyone? Has the whole town gone crazy?"

"Stella. I mean Stephanie. I sort of committed you to a meeting with the director and one of the producers of this possible production. They are negotiating with the publisher for the screen rights and from where I sit it will be a sweet deal for you and to be honest for me," Pamela was using her most persuasive tone.

"Write down the details of when, where, and what time? Do we need to get a lawyer in on this? I have a friend. . . "

"No need. It's all handled," Pamela said. She waved me away with her perfectly manicured hand. This skirmish was over.

"One more thing," I said. "Don't ever contact Harry or Quentin again. This is between you and me and the powers of Hollywood. This town is rattled enough. Don't make it worse."

Her back was turned but I had a feeling that my words fell on deaf ears.

12

By the time I finished my directive to Pamela, we were at the end of Harry's driveway. I could see the trucks from the radio and television stations parked all over downtown. Luckily I had foreseen some of this and parked around the corner. Pamela, however, was not so fortunate. It would be hours before the traffic cleared enough for her to retrieve her vehicle from its illegal space.

Pamela had a look of panic written on her forehead. I pretended not to notice. By the time she realized her predicament I had made my escape but I realized it was only temporary.

Because of the furor in the town, the community college had wisely cancelled class so Quentin was home furiously drafting a contract for Pamela to peruse. Why? I don't know since there wasn't anything tangible to negotiate.

"Quentin, we need to get Sgt. Grimes over here and share our findings. Uncle Harry has information on the murder victim that will be of use in solving the crime."

"Crime. What crime? Ed Lawson died of asphyxiation because the vehicle he was driving was faulty. It says so in the police report."

"But the coroner's report show that Ed's stomach contents reveal that he was poisoned by something containing methanol – maybe moonshine. Who makes moonshine in this area? Any idea? And more importantly why would Ed drink it? Did the one who gave it to him know it was poisoned or was it another accident?"

"What are you saying? We must have proof. We can't just go around saying stuff and accusing people," Quentin responded.

"The notes from Ed's copy of *The Diva Code* point to a mayoral candidate who has a dark secret in his/her past. It also draws implications about a missing sibling, an infant death, and a number of similarities between an influential family and blackmail. Ed's threats were taken seriously by someone and the only way out was to kill him and make it look like either suicide or an accident. Either way, whoever is responsible lives in our neighborhood."

"Well when you put it like that," Quentin replied. "Stephanie, if any part of what you've just said is true, then you are in real danger."

"That's why we've got to turn over all the evidence we have to Sgt. Grimes," I replied.

"Right. Have you noticed anyone following you or acting suspicious?"

"Only Pamela and she has just got on my last nerve," I said with a chuckle, "but the media vans have her so blocked in that she won't be a problem for a while."

++++++

Sgt. Grimes was just as gruff as ever. He wasn't thrilled to see us but then I don't think thrilled is in his vocabulary. He slurped his coffee and barely acknowledged our presence as we poured out the research Quentin had done, my brief encounter with Beth Alewine, Harry's findings, and the suspicious appearance of Ms. Alewine at Ed Lawson's funeral. I mentioned my findings in Ed's copy of my book but neglected to say how I acquired it. As an added bonus, I produced Ed's letters to me. I confessed their presence to Quentin last night and he agreed that they must be submitted as evidence.

Still after all this Sgt. Grimes showed little interest. He downed more coffee and then spoke, "is this part of some publicity stunt to publicize a movie?"

"Absolutely not. There is no movie deal. I haven't signed or agreed to anything. People have gone nuts and I didn't have anything to do with it. I can't say the same for my agent, Pamela Jones. She has gone a little overboard and so have other people close to me," I looked at Quentin who averted my glance.

"Tell me about it," Sgt. Grimes complained. "With the death of Mr. Lawson, the political campaign, and now this furor over what may or may not be a movie deal in our midst, the police can't get much done. We've got traffic jams, long lines everywhere, and people jockeying for publicity for their businesses. . . you name it. This place is chaos."

It was true but I stifled a smile at seeing the confident Sgt. Grimes not in control. For him it was most upsetting but for the rest of us it was amusing.

"You are right of course. But what I want to know is, do you have any information on someone selling or distributing moonshine? I know it is legal under some circumstances, but how do you supposed Ed Lawson who was only in town for a few hours got hold of some?"

Sgt. Grimes got out of his chair and closed the door. He looked both of us in the face and said, "First of all, this conversation never happened, okay? But you and I both know there are 'ways' of getting anything if you know the right folks. I have an idea where the moonshine came from, but I'm wondering if it was poisoned before or after it came from this source. If I make the wrong call, my career is over and as for you two , you might as well start packing."

"That powerful, huh?" Quentin asked.

"That powerful," Sgt. Grimes replied.

"But why? What's the motive? I have a hunch it goes back to Lilith's disappearance in the eighties."

"Who's that?" Grimes asked.

Quentin spoke up, "It's all in the letters. Lilith is Beth Alewine's sister. She mysteriously disappeared after a scandal of some kind."

"Is she dead?" Grimes asked.

"Don't know. But I believe Larry and Beth are covering up for something she is responsible for. Larry may not even know what it is either," I said.

"Well, if he is willing to kill for it, he'd damn well better know what it is and how far he's willing to go," Sgt. Grimes replied. "Money talks but when it comes to crimes of this caliber, it can suddenly get laryngitis." He laughed at his own clever remark.

Quentin and I looked at each other. Maybe it was time to go to state or federal authorities. Especially if this was a crime of passion or involved some deep seated personal or political ties.

We made excuses and headed for home. Now I was really worried. Obviously, the good sergeant knew more than he was willing to say. His job was in jeopardy and the local coroner was a distant Alewine cousin not to mention many more kinfolk on the town council.

On the way home, I confessed to Quentin everything I had been keeping back about Ed Lawson, the notes in *The Diva Code*, the visits to Harry, Beth attending Lawson's funeral service, when I received the letters, and anything else I could think of. He was already aware of most of it but I wanted to make sure we were on the same page.

"I would like for us to sit down and calmly record everything. Before we call in any authorities, we have to appear organized, informed, and rational not like some crazies who see conspiracy and murder at every turn," Quentin said in his most authoritative tone.

I loved him even more when he used his professorial voice. I would follow him anywhere. He was a very wise person and with his help, we could get to the bottom of who killed Ed Lawson and why?

Quentin retrieved the newspaper and the mail from the mailbox. I opened the storm door to put my key into the lock when a note fell onto the door sill.

NOSY PEOPLE DIE

13

Okay now I'm officially worried. Up until now, this had been an exercise in curiosity and justice. Now it was personal. Quentin came up behind me. My hand trembled as I handed him the paper. I wished that I hadn't touched it. Maybe they could get fingerprints but it was too late for that now.

I crumpled into Quentin's arms.

"This has gone far enough," he said. "We need to get protection for you, for Harry, and for everyone involved."

"Now honey, don't overreact. This may be someone's idea of a joke or just an idle threat. There's plenty of sickos out there," I said trying to convince myself.

"You are exhausted. Why don't you let me take this to Uncle Harry. If he can't protect me then no one can. In the meantime, you need to get some rest and focus on your dossier. How does that sound?"

He reluctantly agreed and walked me to my car. Quentin was exhausted mentally and physically. The last few weeks had been a roller coaster. We had a murder on our door step. He found out his wife had a secret career plus she had mail from an admirer. He had to cancel his trip to work on his promotion dossier. And more recently, Hollywood personnel arrived with possible plans for his wife's book, which had been clutched in a dead man's hand. It was over the top emotionally.

I noticed people looking at us differently. Colleagues and friends were more standoffish and held back regular invitations. I worried that promotion and tenure were on the shelf for Quentin. He had worked hard in his chosen profession and now with this furor, God only knows. I prayed that my hobby turned profession wouldn't hinder his dream of becoming a full professor at the college.

On the bright side, book sales were at an all-time high. My agent, star-struck as she was at the moment, was a marketing genius. She had managed color displays in the local book store and the major chain located in the mall. She rallied the town and had banners hung and appointments made.

How she managed to get t-shirts and totes bearing the *Diva Code* logo at such quick notice I'll never know. It was almost embarrassing the amount of publicity I was getting – I said almost.

It was 11:30 p.m. and I dared to telephone Uncle Harry who promptly answered.

"Are you still up?" I asked.

"Of course," he chuckled. "I have to watch the late news to see what's happening in our corner of the world. By the way, who's going to play me in the movie? I was thinking Robert Redford or maybe Sean Connery if he can manage my southern drawl."

"Very funny. Can I come over? I've had a . . . development," I asked.

"Yes. Shall I invite Mr. Coffee? Is it going to be a long night?"

"Perhaps. I don't know yet better make it decaf."

"And Uncle Harry. Did you get a chance to read the letters?"

"Well, as a matter of fact I did."

"Quentin read them today at the police station, but I am not sure how much he understood. I'd like to go over them with you tonight. Is that okay?" I asked.

"You know it is."

14

Like a bolt of lightning I understood what Ed was trying to tell me in his cryptic notes and letters. Just who was Beth's sister, Lilith? I hadn't ever met her. Come to think of it I don't think I had ever seen a picture of her. But Ed had.

Ed had also seen pictures of the Alewines plastered all over town. He had seen promos on television and put two and two together. Just what did he suspect was the connection? How much did he know for a fact? How much did Larry Alewine know?

Uncle Harry traced the ingredients needed for moonshine through his numerous secret liaisons. The only person in town who ordered them in huge supply was none other than the first family of our little burg.

So we have means and opportunity but what of motive? I tagged a sorority sister who now is head of medical records in a southeastern regional facility. She compared two DNA samples that I provided with older ones preserved from the crime scene years ago. A match.

Now thanks to Harry's vigilance and his back up of the poison theory I had everything I needed to go to the authorities.

Harry in his military efficiency has the equivalent to a police murder board. He had staked out where everyone was and what time. We had all the suspects and persons of interest pinned on it plus copies of Ed's notes and where we thought they fit into the timeline.

At 2:00 a.m. Harry and I could no longer come up with any new angles. We agreed to continue tomorrow. I kissed Harry good night and headed to my car. I pulled out of the driveway and that's all that I remember until waking up in a back room somewhere bound and gagged with a pounding headache.

I heard voices in the other room. Loud voices. Familiar voices.

"It was your idea to give him the moonshine," said voice one.

"I didn't know it was poison. I was just being friendly. Better him than me," said voice two.

"You are indeed an idiot," replied voice one. "This means we can be indicted for murder. Some lawyer you are!"

With that I was positive, this was Beth and Larry arguing over who poisoned Ed and why. It was fun to watch. Only one problem. Were they going to kill me too? If it was an accident, they could get off with a lesser charge but not if they murder someone in cold blood – namely me.

Not sure how long I listened to the back and forth diatribe when the doors slammed and I heard vehicles cranking. If only I could get to my purse I could phone 911 and get help. I didn't know where I was but didn't phones nowadays have GPS?

My feet were lashed together but I managed to get up on my knees and then stand straight up. I found a wall light switch and managed to turn it on. I realized then that I was in Larry's campaign office in one of the storage rooms. They wouldn't leave me here for long I had to act fast.

I hopped over to the desk and knocked the telephone off the hook. The operator answered but she couldn't hear me with a gag in my mouth. I managed to turn around and pick up a pencil with my fingers and poke at the numbers. It must have been close enough because a 911 operator came on the line. I made loud noises and grunted into the receiver until I couldn't make any more sounds. All the while I was quoted the consequences for making a prank emergency call.

Finally I sank into the chair when I heard another car drive up. Quickly I doused the light and tried to hide behind a shelf of office supplies. If the Alewines were going to do me in, they had a fight on their hands.

The door opened and I felt a stabbing pain. Then all went black.

15

"I thought you were going to pounce on me with your full body," Harry chuckled.

When I heard Harry's voice I realized I was home. Quentin was massaging my wrists and ankles where the ropes had been. My blouse was wet from all the water that had been forced down my throat. I reached out for the cup. My mouth was dry from the gag.

"Harry you saved the day, you old fox," Quentin said as he squeezed my hand. My mind was still a blur. I remembered being in the storage room but nothing else.

"I did nothing of the kind. I merely followed up on my gut. When Stephanie didn't answer my text, I got worried. She told me about the threatening note. So I took a flashlight outside and saw another set of tire tracks that shouldn't have been there. Two and two my good man. Two and two."

"Well I'm glad you called me so that we got Grimes and his men to round up Beth and Larry. The charges will either be murder or manslaughter," Quentin added. "I don't care as long as Stephanie is okay and they can't hurt anyone else EVER."

My head began to clear and I was dying to ask, "Was Ed's death an accident?"

"I don't know but what I don't get is why did Ed show up here in the first place?" Quentin asked.

"Shall I tell him?" I asked Harry. I nodded and adjusted the ice pack on my neck.

"Because Ed realized that he was the father of the infant in the newspaper article he brought to Larry's office. Ed and his then girlfriend, Lilith, were pregnant. Of course Ed didn't know it and couldn't prove anything until he was released from prison and got DNA testing."

"Lilith was Beth's sister, right?" Quentin asked.

"Yes to hear her tell it, but in reality there is no Lilith. It's just one of the personalities Beth used to worm her way into the good graces of higher ups. Only this time she slipped up and got pregnant. She waited too late to do anything about it and almost killed herself with drugs," I explained.

"Obviously, she was a train wreck. Beth had some friends who stashed her for a while and when she surface she had a full backstory with a sister and everything. She told a lot of lies – really good lies. I even believed she had a sister. But when Ed saw the ads for Larry's campaign, he recognized his old girlfriend and he realized that Lilith and Beth were the same person. I guess it flipped a switch. Wouldn't you say, Steph?" Harry said.

"Ed must have been irate. He got in touch with Larry who knew some or all of the story. He obviously persuaded Ed to calm down and offered moonshine. That's when it went awry and the rest was staged," I said and stretched out on the couch. Poor Ed! He was seeking justice and he got none.

"This has been one crazy roller coaster. Who knew the life of an author could be so exciting?" Quentin said. " Do you think there will still be a movie? After all we solved the crime and have somewhat of a happy ending."

Harry and I looked at each other as if we couldn't believe what had just come out of a brilliant professor's mouth.

"Who knows darling? Hollywood loves a happy ending even if someone turns up dead."

16

As soon as I recovered from whatever the Alewines injected me with, I went to see Beth in prison awaiting trial and sentencing. I was praying that the person I knew years ago before all of the madness would return.

Beth appeared through the door with wrists in shackles. She had on the dreadful orange jumpsuit, which made her look like a skinny carrot. I saw a faint smile cross her lips.

The guard seated her and re-shackled her to the table. We waited until the matron left before either of us said anything.

"On Stephanie. I am so sorry for what we did to you," Beth began. "I never meant for you to get hurt. It was reliving a nightmare of epic proportions. Now my life is over. Larry, Jr. is with his grandparents and I probably won't ever see him again. For certain, my marriage is done along with my career."

"Now Beth just hold on. I understand what and why all of this happened, but if the poisoning was an accident Larry will get off with a lesser sentence and you will just be an accomplice," I tried to sound hopeful. No way would I speak about her son or her marriage.

"Can you ever forgive me?" Beth began to cry. I pulled a tissue from my pocket. They had confiscated my purse in case I was carrying a weapon.

"Of course. I just want my friend back," I said.

I tried to change the subject with talk about my book sales, my star struck agent, and Quentin's dreams of grandeur a movie that probably would never be made. She smiled and even chuckled when I mentioned Sean Connery playing Quentin.

"You have a wonderful husband and a great friend in the Colonel or as you call him Uncle Harry," Beth noted.

"You are so right. Without them I never could have solved any of this. The Colonel has been my secret weapon in my diva books."

"I've read all of them you know," Beth said. "I didn't know you wrote them but now that I DO know it makes perfect sense."

"Which one did you like best?" I asked out of curiosity.

"*Diva's Revenge*," she replied.

"But that one isn't published yet," I said.

"You're not the only one with friends in high places," Beth said and signaled for the guard.

When she turned around to face me, Beth's face was contorted in a sneering. Even her eyes seemed to change color. When she spoke, I knew.

"Lilith?"

"But of course. That ninny Beth and her idiot husband couldn't do anything complicated. I went away for a while but now I'm back. Ed was supposed to take care of me, but he didn't show up so he paid the price for betrayal. I'll play the sniveling part until I'm free of this rap and then you'll experience Diva's Revenge up close and personal."

As the guard clasped Lilith's hands behind her back, she blew me a kiss and winked.

Classic City Murders
Book II
Last Rites

1

It had been a year since Lions Gate Entertainment optioned my first book, *The Diva Code*. Pamela Jones, my literary agent, had calmed down a bit since she realized that from option to the silver screen could take years. I suppose that is a good thing because I couldn't take much more excitement.

Quinton, Uncle Harry, and I managed to put away some pretty devious criminals and right now I needed normal. Quinton took his sabbatical from Rutherford Community College to complete his dossier for tenure. After breakfast, I could count on him to lock himself away in the study until the afternoon. This gave me the perfect environment to begin a sequel to my latest novel, *Diva's Revenge*. I had finally put the murder of Ed Lawson and the conviction of Larry and Beth Alewine out of my mind.

A month into our solitude and life intervened when Quinton was called out of town in his role as police consultant. It was a case where his expertise in the occult was required. I was thankful that we had adopted a fourteen-year-old miniature cocker spaniel to be my companion. Khaki was seventeen pounds of affection. Khaki and I had just finished our morning constitutional. I tossed her a treat and poured a cup of coffee. I unfolded the Herald and gasped at the headline.

EXPLOSION AT RUTHERFORD COMMUNITY COLLEGE – ONE DEAD

As if on cue, my cell rang. It was Quinton. As he began to explain his circuitous route home via layovers and airline changes, his voice was little more than a buzz. I pulled up a dining room chair and sat down monitoring my voice to hide my horror.

I inserted the proper "uh-uhs" so that my husband would be satisfied that I was okay. I didn't need him to worry. I missed him like crazy and would be glad when this particular consulting job was over. It had been long and arduous, entailing lots of travel, ending with a trip to Moscow during which we had had virtually no communication.

After ending what I thought was a believable conversation, I continued scanning the news article for details and was horrified to see the name Dennis Camden. That name was all too familiar. He was a colleague of Quinton's at Rutherford. I didn't know much about the Camdens.

I met Dennis' wife, Mary Ann, once at a faculty wives' event. I wondered how she was taking the shock of her husband's death. Details were sketchy almost nonexistent. Investigation was ongoing. Arrangements pending. There was a statement from the president of the college saying that Dr. Camden was doing research on a special project. Dr. Camden was alone in the lab and working late. Cause of death was unconfirmed, but reading between the lines sounded like the explosion left little to identify.

I remembered Dr. Camden as a quiet, retiring sort. He was older than his younger, beautiful wife. She was a beauty worthy of supermodel status. The lab was in the Keystone Building. It was a spacious facility where Quinton and his colleagues often collaborated on special assignments. It was nothing short of a miracle that more faculty weren't in the building at the time. The newspaper article said the lab was supposed to be empty due to a chemical spill. Odd that Dennis disregarded the warning.

With Quinton in a remote area, I had to rely on whatever details my friends in high places could provide. Sgt. Grimes had been an ally in the Alewine debacle. I had also made a friend who worked in the police evidence room. Could this possibly be linked to the case Quinton was working on? Stranger things had happened.

My mind went back to last year and the crazy Alewine family. Beth aka Lilith was in jail along with her husband, Larry. Could this be some weird payback? She did promise revenge but how could that happen? It wasn't like they were the Mafia. But I wouldn't put anything past that family. Their wealth could buy anything – and I do mean anything.

When the forensic team formally identified the burned remains as that of Dennis Camden, other motives popped into my mind. Quinton said one of Dennis' projects was an enzyme that would neutralize the effects of chemotherapy in cancer patients. What would a drug like that be worth? According to reports, all of Dennis' research was destroyed. I wonder if Dennis had notes in more than one place. Only his closest relationships would know.

I parked downtown and took Khaki for a walk on Rutherford's main campus. We picked up the pace and arrived at the blast zone cordoned off by yellow police tape. The remains were still smoldering. Campus police were redirecting traffic and I was asked to take an alternate walking path. Officials in hazmat suits were rescuing computers and other scientific equipment in order to salvage what results they could.

Tracy had the day off from wrangling the vice presidents children so I made a date to meet her for lunch. Whoops! I forgot no dogs at in the café, so I texted her that we were outside on the patio. Over lunch we talked about what had just transpired. She didn't know Dr. Camden, but she had met him on official occasions at the VP's home when she was caring for the children. Her take on his demeanor was the same as mine.

Tracey remarked, "Wouldn't that be something if there was a big scandal and a lot of bigwigs were involved? I overheard Dr. Fazio tell the VP that there were metallic artifacts found in the lab. I supposed they don't want folks to hear about that. Strange happenings. That's just up Quinton's alley."

Yes and that's just what I'm afraid of. Up to now Quinton's involvement had taken him into other areas of the country. This was too close to home. Khaki and I walked back to where I had parked. I felt I needed a caffeine pick-me-up so I ordered a peppermint latte at the window. Khaki was enjoying the sun while I enjoyed my guilty pleasure. A familiar face caught my attention – Pamela Jones. She was at the glass door speaking with someone. I couldn't tell who. That's strange. Why didn't she let me know she was in town? I thought I was the only one she knew in town. When she saw me, she tried to retreat but I accidently on purpose bumped into her.

"Hey Pamela. I didn't know you were in town. Did you come to see me about the tardiness of my manuscript? Or has the screenplay been commissioned and the movie will be made making us rich beyond our wildest dreams?"

With that last bit I made my voice go higher and higher and waved my arms a bit for effect. It had effect all right. Pamela looked shocked out of her socks.

"Actually none of the above. I had some other business here. Personal business," she said and looked back into Starbucks.

"Oh. Sorry. I just stopped in for a latte and thought I must have missed your call. See you later. Bye."

She hurried away. Whoever she had met with was in the wind.

2

By eleven o'clock in the evening, Quinton hadn't phoned, so I went on to bed. Khaki fell asleep on the sofa. I left her there sprawled on the afghan, snoring quietly. Sometime in the wee hours a warm body slipped in beside me and even in my semiconscious state, I recognized his touch.

"Hi, Love. Did you miss me?" His arms encircled my waist and pulled me close. I nuzzled his caress and answered his kisses with complete surrender. We made love and fell asleep. The glow I felt could light up the room.

The next morning, Quinton was still deep in his dreams. I smiled, remembering his sexual hunger last night. I padded slowly downstairs and made the coffee. Khaki was stretched out full-length on the couch, never knowing her master was home.

"Some watchdog you are," I teased. "I could have had Jack the Ripper in bed with me and you wouldn't have budged."

I pulled on my gym shorts and T-shirt along with my worn Reeboks. I didn't take time to put in my contact lens so I pulled my prescription sunglasses from my purse and covered my unruly hair with a Rutherford College cap. Khaki strained against her lead, strangling and wheezing before settling down to a rhythm.

"Brr. I should have put on my hoodie," I said to no one in particular.

Spring was on its way but mornings were still chilly. Once we got going I would warm up. I concentrated on the beautiful morning of promise. The golden forsythia would be blooming soon along with the apple blossoms whose petals resembled pink snow. I silently wished for a jacket, so we stepped up to a brisker pace to keep warm.

Khaki nosed a Chick-Fil-A wrapper and trotted on. She responded to nature's call at the base of an old dogwood tree. I studied the tree flocked bursting with buds just in time for Easter. How did they always know when to bloom? Dogwoods are so sturdy and their blossoms appear glued to the branches, hardy even against a spring cold snap. We began the home stretch.

Later when I was writing at my desk, I thought about the dogwood blossoms and how much people are like them. Many people are so fragile that they are blown off-course by hardship and tragedy while others remain glued to the branch with celestial cement. These few don't seem to waiver no matter how bad things may get. I wonder if Mary Ann Camden is an apple blossom or a dogwood. For that matter, which one am I?

3

Quinton's circadian rhythm was still so whacked up that he couldn't sleep for more than two hours at a time. I hated breaking the news of Dr. Camden's death to him. Afterward I gave him some privacy in the study.

Dennis' memorial service was short, which was an answer to prayer. Mary Ann was thinner and a little older than I remembered her. Of course, grief can do that to a person. Family shielded her on all sides. President Fazio dismissed classes for today enabling all faculty, staff, and students to attend. And attend they did. The antebellum college chapel bulged at its seams with friends, family, spectators, mourners, and everything in between.

I fortified Quinton with caffeine, but he was still jet lagged. Only once did he nod off during the eulogy; I nudged him before he snored out loud. The Reverend spoke of Dennis' gentle and kind nature, of his unselfish lifestyle, and his devotion to family. The audience dabbed their eyes with damp tissues.

At the graveside, Mary Ann collapsed into someone's arms. My heart broke as we stood in silence during the lowering the casket. I squeezed Quinton's hand. We had barely discussed his trip since the news of Dennis's death engulfed all else.

On our way to the car, we walked hand in hand through the cemetery. Among the tombstones, we stopped short at a broken marker with an archangel sitting atop. Quinton took out a notebook and began scribbling names and copied drawings that were etched into the stone. I stooped and cleared debris away in order to read the name. I was absorbed in my reading until I noticed a pair of leather pumps had joined us. Following them up a black linen skirt, my eyes met a tear-stained face. Mary Ann held out her arms. I hugged her and whispered my sympathies.

Quinton straightened and brushed off his tweed coat to regain his professorial dignity. He extended his hand as I backed out of the way.

"Mary Ann," he said, "I cannot tell you how shocked and deeply sorry I am about all this. As you know Dennis and I were not only colleagues, but friends. It is my desire to help in any way I can."

It had been months since I had seen Mary Ann at a Faculty Wives' Luncheon. Dennis's sudden death had furrowed her cream-colored complexion and lined her beautiful mouth. Silver sparkled in her short dark hair, but it was very becoming to her.

"Thank you so much for coming. I can't tell you what it means to have the faculty so supportive. President Fazio has been a great help," Mary Ann said.

I explained that we were going directly home since Quinton hadn't had a whole night's sleep in three days due to the overseas trip, layovers, and jet lag. We promised to keep in touch. She leaned in and said in a near whisper, "Stephanie, could we lunch together next week? There are some things I'd like to talk over with you."

Trying not to show my surprise, I nodded.

"Thursday noon okay at the bagel shop?" Mary Ann asked and attempted a weak smile. "Thanks a lot, see you then."

She turned on her heels and clicked down the garden walk. Mary Ann Camden was a very attractive woman. And with Dennis' connections and careful planning, I'd wager a very rich one.

4

Entering The Bagelry, I felt out of my comfort zone amid the Bagel Head caps and Bagel Breath shirts. Fortunately, the lunchers were more interested in their bagels and herbal tea than in who entered the shop. Beneath my college sweatshirt, my heart was beating to Sousa's march time. I scanned the room and ducked into a booth in the front corner. I pushed my sunglasses down a bit peering over them just enough to locate a menu. Lost between Turky-Lurky on an egg bagel, Savannah shrimp salad on wheat bagel, or Reuben-o-witz on a rye bagel, I turned the page and discover a whole page of soups and salads.

"Sorry, I'm late," Mary Ann said as she slipped into the booth. "Have you ordered yet?"

"No, I'm still studying the menu. There are so many choices, and I've not been here before."

"Don't bother, "Mary Ann said as she quietly took charge. "Let me order."

It was as much a question as a command. With that she retrieved my menu and walked to the rear of the shop. I noticed how different she looked from the last time I'd seen her at Evergreen Memorial Gardens. She exuded confidence in her designer jeans and long-sleeved jade silk shirt, the expensive ones they sell in the Limited. She wore a matched set of malachite earrings. Jewelry is a hobby of mine and I noted the high quality of the matched stones. Mary Ann had good taste in jewelry and clothes, perhaps even in men. Still she hardly looked the role of the bereaved soul I had expected to find. She looked more like a business professional in her off-duty hours. Her conversation with the waitperson was punctuated with gestures toward our table accompanied by a few nods and smiles. Mary Ann returned to the booth with two blue, steaming ceramic cups.

"What was that all about?" I asked.

"I was ordering us up two House Specials," she said with a smile. "You'll love it. It's my own concoction; a cross between their Sam's Bad Boy and the Georgia Lee's Melt. You aren't vegetarian, are you?"

I shook my head.

"Coffee?" she asked as she slid a mug of hot, black liquid toward me. Mary Ann seemed quite comfortable, not gaunt like other widows I have witnessed. But of course, they were all more than seventy years old! It had been a few days for her to adjust, but if I lost Quinton could I ever recover?

Part of me had not wanted to keep this lunch date, to let it slip my mind, and simply forget to reschedule. But, alas, I am a terrible liar. The exception to that of course is keeping a writing career a secret from Quinton for three years, but that's more of a 'don't ask don't tell' than an actual lie. At least that's how I justified it.

So here I am in a bagel shop at Five Points on a Thursday morning waiting for my House Special, whatever that is, and listening to a newly widowed, almost complete stranger. My mind keeps pouncing from one conclusion to another. I am thankful that we are not on some future ethereal plane where she can read my thoughts.

"I'm glad you suggested that we have lunch. I've been thinking about you ever since the funeral. How are you adjusting to . . . everything?" I held my face quite somber and stirred my coffee with the little plastic striped stirrer. I played with a packet of sweetener and then replaced it in its chrome cradle.

Mary Ann emptied the container of half-and-half into her coffee and stirred it quickly in. Before answering, she raised the cup to her lips and blew the steam as she sipped the hot brew.

"I think I'm still in shock and denial about Dennis's death. I keep going over and over the details, trying to make some sense of it. I constantly search my memory for a clue, a hint, some little something that Dennis said or did."

"Did he get any mysterious telephone calls or notes? Anything threatening concerning the enzyme he was working on?" I asked.

"No. But even if he did, he wouldn't tell me because he wouldn't want me to worry," she answered.

We ate the Bagelry special, which was very tasty. I mentioned Quinton's obsession with football. She commented about the weather. Then Mary Ann asked about my writing which kept me yakking for a while. Thankfully neither of us mentioned the fiasco with the Alewine family.

After we finished the meal and were sipping our second cup of coffee, Mary Ann turned in the booth and began digging in her Gucci purse. I watched her pile a matching wallet, a tissue with red lip prints, a pill bottle, and a half-eaten roll of LifeSavers on the table.

"Here it is," she said as she jammed the contents pile back in their expensive leather home and laid something on the table next to my hand. A black velvet bag which I assumed contained something important.

"I found this in the bedside table. I don't recognize it as belonging to Dennis," she said and emptied the contents onto the table top.

"What does this symbol mean? Is it some kind of occult jewelry? I need some advice as to whether it is important enough to hand over to the police. I thought Quinton, with his expertise, might identify it."

I turned it over in my hand. Some tiny letters were at the base. So tiny I could hardly make it out. I pulled my reading glasses out of my purse to examine it more closely. The clasp at the end of the snakelike silver chain was broken as if it was torn from a neck. Perhaps Mr. Mild Mannered wasn't what he appeared to be.

I shook my head.

"It appears to be some kind of amulet, maybe an antique piece. Can I keep it for a few days and let Quinton research it? He has lots of books on this sort of thing. Maybe he can identify this symbol."

"Sure. Keep it as long as you want. It gives me the creeps to have it around," Mary Ann said.

Mary Ann placed the pendant into its black velvet bag and handed it over. We continued to chat. A passerby would have assumed that we were former sorority sisters. We laughed, took turns showing off family pictures, and relating hilarious stories about our "perfect" vacations. Mary Ann's eyes shone with tears when she told of the last vacation she and Dennis had taken. It was their 30th wedding anniversary trip. Their children had sent them on a cruise to the Bahamas. The pain must have been bittersweet as she recalled their cruise. I listened with hope that some cathartic healing would come of the re-telling.

When the meeting was winding down, I asked Mary Ann, "Has Dennis ever mentioned a Pamela Jones to you?"

Was it my imagination or did her demeanor change? She placed the Gucci bag in her lap as a signal that she was ready to leave.

"No I don't believe so. Dennis and I didn't meet until after graduation, so we didn't share those friendships. Does this person have information about Dennis' death?"

"No. I just was following a hunch about someone being in a place I didn't expect them."

Mary Ann picked up the tab, "I've got this."

When she was paying with a credit card, I slipped her napkin into my tote. You never know when these things will come in handy. What was wrong with me? Did I suspect everyone? Yes.

It had been a two-hour lunch. I had mixed feelings about Mary Ann Camden. Was she what she seemed? Only time would tell.

5

Quinton and I were looking forward to a quiet dinner alone. He lit the gas grill. I prepared the potatoes for baking and washed the salad vegetables. Quinton rubbed the rib eyes in seasoning salt and marinated the meat. I loved our Monday evening cookouts; we had faithfully kept this night for "us" for many years. We had trained everyone not to call, unless it was an extreme emergency. Then the doorbell rang. I looked out the glass doors and saw the neon orange cab glowing like an ember in our neighborhood. Only then did I remember that Uncle Harry had asked to stay with us while his house was getting painted. It had completely slipped my mind.

"Hey Harry!" Quinton's welcome was warm and sincere even if he did wonder what was up. The two men clasped hands. Quinton was a true, southern gentleman in every way.

"Hello, Uncle Harry. So happy you could join us."

I caught Quinton's eye and put my finger to my lips. I mouthed 'explain later.'

"Come in. Here, let me help with your bags," Quinton offered.

"Have you eaten dinner? We were just about to have ours," I added.

"That sounds first rate. Just let me wash up a bit first."

Harry followed Quinton upstairs to the guest room. I heard the thud of suitcases and the closing of doors. Quinton showed him the guest bedroom and bath. They exchanged a few more pleasantries before Quinton came back down the stairs.

"Okay Stephanie. Spill. What is Uncle Harry doing here with suitcases? And on a Monday?"

Before Harry returned to the dining room, I gave Quinton the Reader's Digest version of how he was getting some rooms painted and was going to a hotel when I suggested he stay with us.

We ate our salad, potatoes, and steak kebobs, a quick variation of our two rib eyes. Harry, as usual, entertained us with his adventures in New Guinea, his involvement with the CIA and FBI, and his latest interests in Somalia. Uncle Harry was an amazing man, a "larger than life" character, and someone I totally trusted.

Quinton slipped in a few anecdotes here and there when Harry asked about his Russian trip. We all had a laugh about AEROFLOT food and service or rather the lack of it.

I scooped up the plates and started for the kitchen. Khaki trailed behind me.

"Don't feed her any table scraps. You know what the vet said. They're not good for her," Quinton reminded.

"Just a few bites of steak trimmings. What's it going to hurt?"

Quinton shook his head. He and Harry polished off a slice of cheesecake each. The talking and wildly animated stories continued through dessert. I suggested that we take our coffee into the living room. On our way Quinton's cell phone rang. Harry and I took our mugs of coffee and settled ourselves, he on the couch and I in my rocker.

"Who was on the phone?" I asked and immediately wished I hadn't.

"It was Detective Morrison. He called to ask for my help on a case they're working on -- the Camden case. He asked me to help identify some occult symbols and give him some background. I seem to have somewhat of a reputation as having expertise on the occult and since I'm local, they've sort of pressed me into service." He tried hard to make it sound cut-and-dry, a textbook case to Harry, but I knew better.

"This is decaffeinated, I hope," said Uncle Harry as I poured him another cup. "I can't afford to stay awake tonight. I'm much too tired."

"I'm afraid decaf is all poor Quinton gets unless we are at a restaurant," I said.

After nodding off twice during our conversation, Uncle Harry made his excuses and headed upstairs to bed. Quinton left for the police station. I put the dishes in the dishwasher, wiped the counters, and locked up. Everything else could wait until morning.

Only after going upstairs did I remember the amulet. I felt in my pocket to make sure it was still there. I placed it in my bedside table. Well after midnight, Quinton returned home and slid in beside me after he pushed Khaki to the foot of the bed and turned off the light. Peace at last.

6

Morning jolted me back into the real world of errands, cleaning, and bill paying. After my shower, I found Uncle Harry happily grazing away on Honey-Nut Cheerios and watching reruns of "I Love Lucy."

"Why don't they make stuff like this anymore? This show is hilarious," he said while I made a grocery list. I smiled and nodded, but made no comment. The question was rhetorical. .

"Is there anything you need at the store, Harry?" Harry looked thoughtful for a moment and shook his head. He was much too involved with the Ricardos and Mertzes than with the real world. I guess he deserved to "veg" for a while.

"Quinton should be down any minute. He's not teaching today but doing research at the library." Whoops I almost said too much. No matter, Harry was only listening to about every third word and mindlessly munching his cereal. His brain would be as soggy as that cereal if he kept watching "I Love Lucy" reruns.

I mentally checked off my errands and grabbed my purse. Quinton circled my waist.

"Hi, beautiful. Where are you off to today?" He said. "Is Harry going with you or is he holding court here?"

"Oh, His Majesty is indeed up watching "I Love Lucy" reruns and eating your stash of Honey-Nut Cheerios," I said. "You'd better hurry if you expect to get any cereal this morning."

"Has the Colonel given any indication when the painters will be finished?"

"No. I haven't mentioned it yet, but I think it will be soon. This afternoon, he plans to check on his greenhouse with all his lovely poisonous plants. Harry is concerned that the fumes will harm them. He nurtures them more than some folks do their children," I said.

"Hey don't bite the hand. Remember, he's your poison expert," Quinton reminded me.

"I know. I know. And that's a task I need to get back to. Pamela is screaming for the book and I have writer's block – big time."

"Now for my share of the Honey-Nut goodness," Quinton said.

"Wait! Have a look at this." I handed him the amulet that Mary Ann gave me.

"Where did you get this?" Quinton asked.

"From Mary Ann Camden. She gave it to me when we had lunch. She found it in Dennis' bedside table. Do you think that it's important?"

"It might be. Let me take it to the research library and see what I can find."

"There's something else. A few days before the accident, Dennis phoned and asked for you."

"Really, you didn't mention it.?"

"I suppose in all the excitement I forgot. He was very polite and didn't leave a message."

I grabbed my purse and jacket and waved.

"Bye all," I said as I threw my purse strap over a shoulder. Quinton looked up from his Cheerios long enough for a smile and a wave. Eating cereal and watching TV, my husband looked like a big Dennis-the-Menace with a blonde lock refusing to cooperate with the rest of his hair.

8

I knew that when I gave Quinton the amulet, he would spend whatever it took to get to the bottom of what it meant and where it came from. When we had a moment alone, he mentioned similar objects being left across town at the scene of other crimes.

Quinton was a dedicated researcher. I knew that at given time he could be found in the special reference section of the Rutherford College library. Or if not there, he was in his home office digging through books of spells, symbols, occult and Gothic literature, or on the Internet gleaning information. He was constantly updating his knowledge of the occult both for his classes and for the police consultant position. Sometimes he discussed with me what modern pagans and the popular "do-it-yourself" religious groups were into. I was appalled at what these groups were capable of.

Quinton was not foolish. He'd had dealings with witchcraft and pagan groups before. Many neopagans enrolled in the Gothic literature and New Age religion classes that he taught. Even if they didn't agree with him, they admitted his presentation were fair.

The Colonel aka Uncle Harry was also quite fond of Khaki. Uncle Harry lost his faithful Norwegian Elkhound, Spud, and never gotten over it. I came back from errands and Harry was outside with Khaki. When he threw the ball for Khaki to fetch, I interrupted their game.

"Uncle Harry, do you know anything about the occult?" I asked.

"I've read up on potions made from the plants in my greenhouse. Cults and the occult use poisons in their curses. Sometimes they coat various amulets with toxins, as well as sacrifice animals, which of course is out of my area of expertise. Why do you ask?"

"I know you heard about the lab explosion, Dennis Camden's death, and all the rumors that have been circulating," I said.

"Oh I don't pay attention to rumors. Facts are much more delicious," Harry said with that quirky sense of humor that I love.

I pulled out my cell phone and showed Harry a picture of the amulet that we had been researching. He enlarged it, looked at it from different angles, and handed it back.

"Not sure. But it seems to be some kind of Wiccan charm. Quinton could look it up in the one of the grimoire volumes, probably the Lesser Seal of Solomon," he said matter-of-factly.

"You never cease to amaze me," I said and hugged him. "I try."

9

It had been over three weeks since Dennis' death. Two weeks since Mary Ann and I ate lunch at the bagel place. I questioned whether I should call her and invite her to have coffee. We didn't have much information yet on the amulet, but I was anxious to see how she was adjusting. The last thing I needed to do was concern her about Dennis' possible connection with the occult.

At the same time, Harry got the okay to move back to his digs and President Fazio asked Quinton to teach a class in Atlanta for a colleague who had the flu. We agreed that he should spend the night since the class ran late. So with the house empty, I replaced the frozen ground beef I designated for spaghetti and opted for a frozen dinner. I rubbed Khaki's head.

"It's just you and me tonight, old girl," I said. After dinner, I went upstairs to work on the Diva sequel. Editing was my least favorite thing but I got through the manuscript one more time.

"Enough for tonight, girl," I said to a snoring cocker spaniel who was decidedly not interested in my writing career. Whether it was the grinding whine of a forced lock or the thud of something pushed against a wall, I can't say, but the sound roused me and telegraphed a clear message. An intruder was in the house!

Frozen by fear, I lay silently in my king-size bed. Frantic ideas raced through my barely conscious mind. What should I do? Where is my phone? In what part of the house was the intruder? What were they after? I glanced at the digital clock on the night table -- 3:00 A.M. I had only come to bed around midnight, when I finished editing *Diva's Vendetta*.

Slipping out of bed, my pupils dilated, adjusting to the dark. I opened the bedroom door and peered down the hall - no lights, nothing. Then it came again. I could tell from the resonance that it came from the lower part of the house—Quinton's study.

My feet felt around for my slippers. I grabbed the robe at the foot of the bed and threw it on. I managed the stairs slowly and made my way into the living room. Stumbling across the room dimly lit by a tiny night-light; I nearly fell over Khaki who apparently changed positions when I went upstairs. She never stirred. I groped my way to the end table, grabbed my cell, and dialed 911. Why hadn't I brought the cellular phone upstairs like I usually do?

The police arrived within minutes. My neighbors awakened to the noise of police cars, lights flashing in all directions, and our subdivision being turned into chaos. The police searched the premises, took a lot of notes, dusted for fingerprints and packed up. Sargent Grimes, now a detective, was as gnarly as ever. He remained to fill me in on the details, which were blurry at best.

After the hubbub settled down, I was too tense to go back to bed. The police found no fingerprints, but the lock appeared to have been jimmied. Plus a dining room chair overturned. However, nothing was broken or missing that I could determine. I would go over my list of valuables and check the lock box tomorrow. Quinton would be able to spot anything missing more quickly than I could.

Quinton's prized antique roll-top desk was intact; however all the desk drawers gaped open with their contents strewn around. The middle drawer was closed -- either stuck or locked but the key slot was scratched. I never noticed that before. I don't even know where Quinton keeps the key? Only he would know if this was new or had always been there.

Sitting at the dining room table with a cup of strong black coffee, I witnessed the orange sunrise against the beautiful Georgia pines and steadied my nerves. Another day is dawning in the red clay country. The break-in alarmed me more than I wanted to admit. Maybe Grimes was right. He surmised it was someone looking for drugs or cash. It was too invasive to be a prank. But why overturn a damask chair or throw papers around? His theory made no sense, but I didn't even have a theory. Someone somewhere was intensely interested in our personal lives. Someone was watching and knew I would be home alone. Someone. But who?

I thought about telephoning Quinton. But there was nothing he could do. Why wake him when he would be home from Atlanta in a few hours?

I've never been afraid to stay by myself or to be alone before, but so much has happened in the last few months. I feel as if I'm being watched maybe even toyed with. Perhaps this was a warning to me. Or was Quinton the one in real danger?

Khaki bounded into the room, found her chew bone, and settled into a corner. Why didn't she bark last night? She couldn't HEAR an intruder but weren't her other senses supposed to be heightened? What if, and this thought terrified me, she recognized the intruder and didn't bother to warn me?

The alarm on my phone went off and startled me. I must have dozed off. I washed my face in warm water and put some saline in my eyes. I forgot to take my contacts out and they felt like sandpaper. I remembered some left over pizza in the fridge and decided to heat it up. When I reached the kitchen and was microwaving the leftovers, the phone rang. Quinton was on his way home and remembered that he had a faculty meeting.

I blurted out, "Someone broke into the house last night."

"What! Are you okay?" His voice raised and alarm was apparent in his tone.

"I'm okay. But your study was the target of the break in. Grimes was here. We checked everything the best we could. I couldn't tell if anything was missing. Papers and books were strewn around. Another thing. There were scratches on your desk drawer; it looks like they tried to break the lock. Maybe they were trying to scare you, or me. But just maybe they were after whatever information you might have on the Camden murder."

"I'm coming straight home. Damn the faculty meeting. I can't take a chance of someone harming you. I didn't want to alarm you before I left, but Stephanie, your hunch was right. Dennis' death wasn't an accident. Dennis was murdered."

"Murdered!"

The one word I didn't want to hear. I felt dizzy, nauseous, and afraid all at once. Still I didn't want Quinton to be alarmed.

"Grimes is a detective now. He has his men patrolling. They brushed for fingerprints and still searching for evidence."

"I wonder why that doesn't make me feel better. The force hasn't been able to put away the rapist that's been terrorizing Five Points lately. How can I hope that he could track down a killer? Did you get in touch with Harry?"

"No I didn't want to worry him. But when I asked Uncle Harry about the occult, he is a lot more knowledgeable than I gave him credit for. Really, dear, go on to the faculty meeting. I'm not afraid. I'm having all the locks changed today and installing a burglar alarm. Uncle Harry will come over as soon as he hears. Really. I'm fine. You just finish up and come home as soon as you can."

"Well, if you're sure."

"I'm sure. I love you."

"I love you, too. The meeting shouldn't run too late. I'll bring home Chinese. You just relax and get those locks and alarms taken care of."

With all of the tasks taken care of, I went to retrieve the mail. A few clouds, maybe it will rain. I sifted through the water bill, ad circulars, pizza handbills, and another from the Superior Court of Clarke County. Perfect! I have jury duty. It just gets better and better. What next?

10

The stars, sun, moon and planets must have aligned because my two besties, Carol and Doris, were also summoned for jury duty. Meeting up with them at the court house took the edge off jury duty and gave us plenty of time to catch up during the interminable wait. In olden days they let us bring our knitting, but no more. I suppose they fear an ornery jury member stabbing another with a knitting needle. After all they are pointy things. The guards also scan our purses and confiscate our cell phones so Words with Friends was out.

Doris, Carol, and I were all accepted and I didn't know if that was a good thing or not. We'd get a little pocket money but with parking fees, gas, and lunch I hoped to break even. When the jury wasn't deciding someone's fate for jaywalking, or being too close to the school with crack cocaine, or listening to some half-baked story, I jotted down possible story lines for the next two Diva books. My idea was that when my character will have run their course in the Diva series, I will need another mystery series with a unique twist. Yeah. Good luck with that one. As Solomon observed, 'there's nothing new under the sun.'

I prayed this whole jury thing wouldn't tie me up all week, but the bright side was that at lunchtime I could run my ideas by Doris and Carol. We talked at lunch, then I emailed the copy, and the next day they'd give me feedback on what worked and what didn't. Fresh eyes were always a good thing as far as writing goes, but they can't be ones that are afraid to hurt your feelings. I learned long ago that your spouse or your mother can't be unbiased when it comes to critiquing your writing.

The third day of jury duty we were dismissed and thanked for our services. And given "the check is in the mail" speech. I got home a little early. Quinton was still in class, but the message on my desk said to telephone him when I got in. Jury duty puts you out of touch with the universe. It's kind of like being held hostage.

"Hi Honey, what's up?" I cooed when Quinton picked up.

"Hey Stephanie. I wanted you to know that somehow Grimes got wind of the occult factor and asked me what I knew. Of course, I had to come clean about the amulet and what I'd found out thus far which isn't much. He made me surrender it but I took a picture of it with my phone before I did."

"Wow. And I was having such a good day," I said.

"He may question you about how you got the amulet and so on. Just tell the truth. He knows and just wants to check my story. I take it that the police still don't have a clue about Dennis' death." Quinton continued, "Both the good sergeant, I mean the detective, and I came to the conclusion that the break-in the other night was all about finding the amulet. Fingerprints were smudged or nonexistent. The forced lock was done by an amateur according to the police investigators. Thank God you didn't catch them. Who knows what might have happened?"

"I know I try not to think about it. Whoever broke in didn't know we had a dog, or if they did, they knew Khaki couldn't hear well. I wonder if that's a clue," I wondered out loud.

"Stephanie we are not characters in one of your books. This is real. You were in danger, understand?" Quinton said in a tone I was not familiar with.

"Yes. I do"

"Think. Did anyone see Mary Ann give you the amulet? Did you show it to anyone else? Did you mention it to anyone? This is important," Quinton's said sternly.

"I don't think so. Of course, I didn't know what she was about to give me and there were other people eating at the Bagelry. I didn't show it to anyone or tell anyone, but if someone SAW her give it to me I couldn't be sure. Do those places have cameras? You know in case of a robbery or something? Maybe Grimes could flash his badge around and find something captured on tape," I said trying to sound light-hearted.

"Please be serious. I have another class. I have to go. I'll be home soon. Oh and I almost forgot Uncle Harry is trying to get in touch with you. Love you. Bye."

11

I told Siri to dial Uncle Harry but he didn't pick up. It went straight to voice mail. Sometimes he forgets to take his cell into the greenhouse, so I drove home to take off my 'jury clothes' and put on something more comfortable like shorts and a tee shirt.

With jury duty over, I had a few ideas I wanted to jot down before they floated into cyberspace. A lot of my ideas do that. I complained so much that Quinton bought me a pen that lights up so I can write down ideas in the middle of the night without switching on an overhead light. If only I could remember where I put the thing!

I made a sandwich and tried Harry again. Surely he'd clipped, weeded, fed, and watered all his poisonous garden plants by now. The doorbell rang but I didn't get there quick enough to view who rang it. I looked down and there was a note folded neatly on the welcome mat.

DO YOU KNOW WHERE YOUR DOG IS?

Panic went through every being of my body and I began searching the house and calling Khaki even though I realized she probably couldn't hear me. I went through every room, out to the back yard and finally out the front door.

For a brief moment I thought I heard a rustle in my rose garden. Though I was almost too afraid to look, I took a hoe from the garage and pulled back the thorn bushes. There was Khaki panting and frothing at the mouth. With no regard for the thorns, I ran inside grabbed my keys from the table and scooped her into the van. If I had a siren, I would have used it.

Please, God, don't let Khaki die was my first thought and my second was, *Who did this and why?*

12

In the veterinarian's waiting room I tried Harry's cell again. This time he answered.

"Uncle Harry, are you okay? You sound out of breath."

"Hey yeah. I'm okay. I must have been rearranging the pots in my greenhouse when you called. I think I got carried away and lost track of the time, then I was starving, and made lunch. It was only after I had devoured half of my Weight Watchers French Bread Pizza before I noticed that I had a message," Harry said.

I had a mental picture of Uncle Harry on his loveseat with a bottle of Chianti on the coffee table and French Bread Pizza on a silver tray in front of him. Weight Watchers should get him to do a television commercial. I looked at my watch. It was time for Harry's soaps along with his wine therapy which, according to him, prolonging his life. Harry was an original and I hoped he never changed.

"I wanted to let you know that someone tried to poison Khaki, but don't panic. I got her to the vet in time and she'll be okay. I'm trying to find out what was used, how, and why. Naturally, I thought of you."

"I can't say the words I'd like to because you are a lady, but when and I say when, not if, we find out who did this, I want some time alone with him," Harry said.

"Or her," I interjected. "We can't rule out anyone. Remember Beth Alewine?"

"True, so true. Wait just a second. Not you, Stephanie."

"Harry is someone with you?"

"Yes I had a friend over but she's leaving now. Get all the facts you can from the vet and high tail it over here. I want to get this bastard ASAP," Harry commanded.

"Aye Aye," I said and almost smiled. Did Harry say *she*?

If I weren't so horrified about Khaki being poisoned, I would have done a little dance. But as it was I wasn't in any mood for dancing. I waited for the vet's report and got to see poor Khaki laid on a table with tubes everywhere. She looked as if she had expired but the dog doc assured me that she was recovering nicely after having a gastric lavage. I know what that means even if he was trying to soften the blow. The vet wanted to keep her overnight for observation. After I whispered "good bye" to her, I grabbed the report and floored it to

Harry's. On the way I phoned Quinton and left a message. I knew he would be in class but would check Whats App on his smart phone when class was over.

The only thing that would ease the picture of my suffering pet was the revenge I would wreak on the one who did it. I knew my partner in retaliation would be Uncle Harry. He was very fond of Khaki and even entertained the notion of adopting her. His drawback was the greenhouse and fear that she would encounter the poisonous residents who lived there.

Harry lives at the end of a cul-de-sac with very little traffic. A perfect place for a semi-hermit who dabbles in secrets. I seldom see cars coming from the direction of his house but today was an exception – a white VW bug complete with a driver swathed in a black scarf and sunglasses. Obviously female and quite obviously visiting Harry.

13

Okay. Stephanie. Don't pry I said to myself. Even if I am the nearest thing Uncle Harry has to family. He is a grown man. He will tell you if and when he wants you to know. Remember you've got bigger fish to fry. There's the Camden murder and of course, Khaki's poisoning. I had this conversation with myself as I pulled into Harry's driveway and climbed the porch steps.

"So Harry. Who's your visitor?" I blurted out.

"What?"

Harry had his back to me. He was straightening sofa cushions and gathering up what was an obvious lunch for two.

"Who's your lunch date?" I reworded the question that I swore not to ask.

Colonel Harry Roberts pulled himself up to his full height – about 5 foot 6 inches I would guess – and looked into my eyes.

"Darling Stephanie. I love you like the daughter I was never privileged to have. But I must tell you this. I am eighty-seven years of age, retired from the United States Army, and do not need your permission to have a friend over for lunch," Harry said in a stern voice I'd never heard before.

"Oh I am so sorry. I didn't mean to pry. I guess I am used to looking out for you and this female lunch date is new territory for me. Please forgive me," I said with the most pitiful voice I could muster.

"Forgiven. Move on."

Harry's tone was unusual and it struck to the heart. I choked back a tear and handed him the report from the veterinarian. He took it and never looked me in the face. Why was Harry hiding his relationship from me?

Harry put on his pince-nez spectacles that I said make him look like Agatha Christie's *Hercule Poirot*. But there was no humor in his soul today. I had upset him with my nosiness. Even though Uncle Harry hurt my feelings, he was absolutely within his rights to entertain whomever he wished with or without my knowledge. And he certainly didn't need permission from anyone.

Even though Harry was older he was in tip top physical condition with only a few wrinkles. He obviously dyes his hair, but he is an attractive guy. I can understand being lonely, I just worry about gold diggers and that sort. Lesson learned: I overstepped my bounds when I inquired about his visitor. That rascal said "she" on purpose just to tweak my nose.

"Looks like the poison used was nicotine," Harry mused.

"Nicotine! You mean like the ingredient in tobacco?"

"Yes. Nicotine is highly poisonous in the right dose. Unfortunately, nicotine is often employed as concentrated tobacco juice and mixed with other liquids to produce pyrethrum, a popular insecticide especially against rose aphids."

I gulped and tears flowed. "Oh poor Khaki. She was lying under the rose bush when I found her."

Harry paid no attention to my feminine outburst and continued, "according to this it was a small dose administered through a dog treat of some kind. Clearly it was to make her sick but not intended to be deadly."

Harry then added another fun fact. "This particular tobacco from which the nicotine was extracted is only grown in one place in the world – Saint James Parish, Louisiana. It is a rare heirloom type of tobacco used exclusively for *Perique* brand cigarettes. Hmmm. Interesting."

I heard what Uncle Harry was saying but I felt the need to rant.

"Who could do this?" I wailed. "Khaki is the sweetest animal in the world. She wouldn't hurt anyone or anything."

"Someone who wanted to hurt you and warn you to keep your nose out of whatever you're snooping in," Harry matter-of-factly answered. "But let it be known, that we will hunt them down and punish whoever has hurt my girls."

With that Harry rose and gave me a big bear hug. I knew I was forgiven for my blunder and all was right with the world, or at least it WOULD be.

"Uncle Harry is there anything I can do for you while I'm here?" I said trying to make up for being a clod.

"As a matter of fact, would you take the recycling to the curb? The old knees are acting up a bit," he answered.

"Of course, I'll do it on my way out. Love you," I called.

"Love you too," Harry answered.

I shouldered my tote and picked up the bin. It wasn't until I sat it on Harry's curb that I noticed a cigarette pack labeled *Black Perique*. Harry's female visitor was a dog poisoner and I am pretty sure I know who she is.

14

In a small town like ours, it isn't too hard to spot an out of town vehicle even if said vehicle is rented. I got my two sidekicks, Doris and Carol, on the lookout for the VW Bug I had seen whizzing out of the direction of Harry's house.

It didn't take long for the two sleuth sisters to find the car and the one who rented it.

"Hello this is Stephanie," I said as my phone chimed.

"Doris, here," the voice came back. "We've found the driver. It's your agent, Pamela. The funny thing is she rented the car under another name."

"Probably under her agency's name so that she can take it off her taxes," I said.

"No. Not at all. She rented it under the name of Pamela Ford. Another thing. The papers list the added driver as Raymond Ford. Is she married and uses Jones as her professional name?" Doris asked.

"Good question. Nice work, girls. You can back off now and let the authorities handle it." And with that I hung up and dialed Quinton. He was finished with class and at home eating a bologna sandwich. I relayed the events of the morning including Harry's secret lunch date and what the girls found out about the owner of the car.

"Did they happen to get a plate number? Or did they find out for sure it was a rental?" he asked.

"It's a rental but under another name. Can you use your consulting connections to see why Pamela is using an alias? Meanwhile I am going to try and find out why she's here. After all I am the only client she has here. Is she pumping Harry for information? I will personally strangle her if she breaks his heart."

"My dear, must I remind you that Harry is a grown man. He is wise beyond our years. He's come through major wars so I think he'll be able to handle a male-female relationship without any help."

"You'd think so wouldn't you?" I responded. "Unfortunately, past history has taught me differently. One look from a beautiful woman and a man's brain freezes. His libido takes control and it's all over."

"Please. Harry isn't an acne pocked teenager with a crush. He's a retired colonel and has led armies into war," Quinton reasoned.

"My statement stands. We have to keep an eye on him for his own sake. Even though it's Pamela. I don't trust any female sniffing around. She's young enough to be his daughter or maybe granddaughter.

"Geez, Stephanie. Give it a rest," Quinton said as he banged off to his office at the police department.

"Mama always said, 'there's no fool like an old fool." There I got in the last word even if Quinton wasn't listening anymore. Getting the last word is important. Ask anyone who's married.

"Carol, this is Stephanie. Can you and Doris meet me at the Java Station?"

"Sure. Are we going to do a stake out?" she asked.

"No. More of a surveillance, but I need help," I told her.

"Goodie. I can finally use my new night goggles and Doris has those new-fangled binoculars with extra distance. We'll be there lickety-split."

"Thirty minutes will be fine. We have to come up with a schedule and a plan. By the way, do either of you have a camera?"

15

"Hello Stephanie, where are you?" Quinton said when I answered his call.

"Oh it's just the background music. I'm at Java Station with Carol and Doris. We're working on story ideas."

Doris raised her eyebrows. I avoided her stare.

"Something interesting has just occurred to me when I was identifying the occultic materials from some of the other cases. The amulets, charms, and miscellaneous objects that were left at other crime scenes are a potpourri of the occult. None of them match. Some are from Wicca, some from Satanic cults, and others are Egyptian artifacts. All are copies of course. There's no one source. Whoever scattered these around had no idea what they were doing. It seems to me that this person or persons was leading the investigators off course by introducing a paranormal factor. None of this stuff looks legit," Quinton's voice sounded confident in his findings.

"So if that's true, then Dennis' murder had nothing to do with the amulet. And Mary Ann finding it has nothing to do with solving his death," I was thinking out loud.

"Then why did she keep it a secret from the police and hand it over to you?" Quinton finished my thought.

"Exactly. Was she trying to help or throw me off the scent?"

"I know you want to be friends with Mary Ann Camden, but is it possible that she's not what she appears? Maybe we need to look further into her background. Do you agree?" Quinton knew my hesitancy since Mary Ann came to be for friendship.

"Yes and I have something that will help," I confided.

* * *

With prints lifted from a lip blot on a napkin, Grimes' cronies discovered that Mary Ann Camden was originally Mary Campbell from Marietta, Georgia. She attended the University of Georgia and was apparently a classmate of Beth Alewine. Sorority event pictures link them at several fund raisers, ball games, and social events.

Quinton and I discussed the findings with Harry.

"But," Uncle Harry pointed out, "that's not enough to link her to anything illegal."

"Mary or Mary Ann as we know her was married for a short time to a George Whitlock when she first graduated from UGA. No children. She married Dennis five years ago. He had children from a previous marriage. His wife died from cancer. That's all I can glean from the police findings," Quinton said.

"Well that's more than I knew." I added. "From all evidence, I believed they had been married for years and years. She referred to the offspring as though they were hers, but of course she would wouldn't she?" I caught myself babbling and feeling bad that I suspected Mary Ann of anything untoward.

"What about Pamela Jones? Can you dig up anything on her?" I said it before I even thought.

"Why would you suspect your agent of any wrongdoing? She's such a lovely sweet thing," Harry purred.

"Uh . . . well, the thing is that I have seen her around town and I was wondering about the reason. I'm the only client that she has, but both times I've spotted her, she was surprised. I just thought that it was strange, unless she was friends with someone else in town," I said without looking in any particular direction.

"I thought you might say that so I took the liberty of asking Grimes to check her out as well. Looks like Pamela is who she says she is. The website gives her credentials and background in being an entertainment agent. But there is an entry that gives a different last name for her."

"What name is that?" Uncle Harry asked.

"Lawson. Pamela Lawson Jones. Do you think it is a coincidence that her maiden name is the same as the guy involved in the Beth Alewine case?" Quinton asked no one in particular.

"Absolutely not," I answered. "On the other hand, maybe it's a fluke. After all she was my agent before any of this stuff about Ed or the Alewines or Dennis ever came up," I was again defending someone that I obviously didn't know very well.

"Let's brainstorm. What if Ed told Pamela his plan before you even started to seek out an agent or a publisher? Pamela recruited you as a client, the book was wildly successful. Pamela was making money so she was thrilled," Quinton said. He was excited that the puzzle pieces were beginning to fall into place.

I was processing what Quinton had proposed as to why Pamela was so interested in our little burg and us in particular.

"Uncle Harry. You are strangely quiet," I said.

He sat as his computer desk and stared ahead. "I suppose you think I've been a fool," he said quietly. "I wanted to believe that Pamela liked my company, but she was just using me like she used everyone else. But there was the smoking thing, too. I never liked being with a woman who smoked. Now I find out that she's married. That's just icing on the cake."

"But Uncle Harry. You provided the link to who poisoned Khaki. It was Pamela's weird brand of cigarettes that produced the poisonous nicotine. I found the cigarette pack in your recycling and that put me onto her as the poisoner. So you actually cracked the case. Without that we'd still be in the dark."

"Really?" Harry said and brightened somewhat. He then added, "You mean to say that Pamela poisoned Khaki? I'll strangle her myself."

"Now hold on. You couldn't possibly know that when you were seeing Pamela. And none of us knew about the link between Pamela and Ed. But the question remains: What's the link between Pamela and Mary Ann? What's the motive? Revenge for Ed? Maybe for Pamela but not for Mary Ann." As I said this Quinton got that look in his eye.

"Ed wanted revenge for his unborn child. Pamela had to feel some of that, but was she willing to go as far as murder? I think there's an aspect we've overlooked."

"What might that be?" Harry was more than interested now. I was afraid he would load his elephant gun and take to the streets.

"Greed," Quinton answered.

16

"Greed, you say?" Harry muttered. "I don't follow. Pamela isn't rich but she dresses pretty expensively. And that Camden woman looks like she stepped out of *Vogue*."

"True, but Dennis was rather conservative with his money. Some said stingy even. And if Mary Ann didn't come from wealth, which we know she didn't, how did she manage such a wardrobe not to mention her jewelry?"

Quinton punched some numbers into his I-phone and asked for the Chief of Police. I gave him that stare that says 'what'? He said into the receiver, "I need to request financials on Mary Ann Camden and Pamela Lawson Jones as persons of interest in the murder of Professor Dennis Camden. I am on my way to sign the paperwork. Thank you."

"Who were you talking to?" I asked.

"Sonya, the secretary to the Police Chief," Quinton answered. "She handles all of the paperwork for the consultants. I have a right to view all necessary items relating to the case. And I think this is pretty important. You've always told me that secretaries run the world, and you my dear are so right. On my way, keep digging and I will let you know what I find."

Quinton left us and I felt that Harry needed a pick-me-up so I suggested we get coffee at the Java Station. If we were lucky, Doris and Carol might see the car and give us an update on their surveillance. It was almost comedic to see those two with their spy gear. They were onto Pamela like white on rice.

Harry commandeered a table while I put in our orders. But who do you think came sashaying over to the table but the famous agent, Pamela Jones. I thought steam would come out of Harry's ears. Ignoring obvious signals, she proceeded to pull up a chair and attempt a conversation.

"You hussy," Harry shouted. All eyes went in that direction. "How dare you act like you care for me and behind my back poison a defenseless animal!"

Louder, Harry I don't think they heard you in the next town. Please Harry. Self-control. The entire population of Java station was now enrapt in the scene being played out before them.

"Why Harry. Whatever are you talking about? With that she pulled out a pack of *Perique* cigarettes and suddenly remembered that this was a no smoking zone. She put them away but not before Harry spotted them.

The sight of the cigarette pack made Harry smolder. He stood up and for a moment I thought he would strike Pamela. She took the hint, grabbed her purse, and made a hasty exit almost running over Doris and Carol.

"Damn, do they serve Scotch in here?" Harry bellowed. I hurried to the table with the coffee orders and tried to soothe Harry's wounded soul.

"Calm down dear. Here have your latte, you'll feel better," I said to my favorite person in the world who looked at me like I had suddenly turned green.

"The only thing that will make me feel better is to feed that woman some candy laced with poison and let her see what Khaki went through," he muttered. "Anyone who would do that to a defenseless animal is not worth my time of day. I'll see to it that she pays. Yes sirree, Bob! If it's the last thing I ever do."

Doris and Carol were still in the doorway trembling from all the excitement. When Carol went to grab two bottles of water I slipped a note to Doris telling her that Pamela was onto us and that she was extremely dangerous. I knew that wouldn't slow them down so I included a listening/locator device so I could keep track of my friends.

They waved a goodbye to us, but Harry was in no mood for anything congenial. He was on the defensive and hurt from the deception. I admonished them to go straight home but I knew that they wouldn't let go of this. They wanted to be in for the take down.

I sipped my peppermint latte quietly and decided to leave Harry to his thoughts. Since Pamela knew that all of us were onto her. She would be out of town before we could notify the authorities. I texted Quinton to have Grimes pick Pamela up as she left town. Harry had put the 'fear of God' into her. We needed her to spill the beans about what had transpired between her and Mary Ann or Beth or whoever she was in cahoots with. Pamela was a smart cookie but somehow I didn't think she was the architect of Dennis' death.

My cell signaled a message from the vet. Khaki was cleared to go home. I showed it to Uncle Harry who immediately brightened.

"What are we waiting for? Let's go get our girl," Harry said and practically vaulted to the door.

17

While Harry and I retrieved Khaki form the vet, Quinton took all of the evidence we had amassed to Grimes at the Police Station. Grimes dispatched uniforms to pick up Ms. Camden for questioning.

We dropped Khaki at Tracey's house. She agreed to dog sit while we were at the station. Grimes permitted Quinton, Harry, and me to be in the room with the two-way mirror while Mary Ann was questioned.

"State your full name for the record please," Grimes said. "This testimony is being recorded."

"Mary Ann Camden," she responded.

"What was your maiden name?"

"Mary Ann Campbell."

"Were you married before you met and married Dennis Camden?"

"Yes. I was married to George Whitlock."

"What happened to Mr. Whitlock?"

"He died."

"Where did you meet Professor Camden?"

"At Rutherford College where I was working as an administrative assistant."

"When was that?"

"Six years ago."

"Did Dr. Camden give you an allowance after you were married?"

"Yes. Why do you ask?"

"Because your spending on personal items is much more than what you husband deposited every month."

"I have other sources of income. I am a licensed life coach and I dabble in interior decorating."

Mary Ann was obvious grasping for answers. She showed a slight flush beginning at her neckline.

"According to your bank records, about a year ago you began receiving large sums of cash on the fifteenth of the month. We traced the source and it began around the time of city elections. Do you want to comment on that?"

"No. It must be a coincidence."

"Well another coincidence is that the same amount every month began to be deducted from Beth Alewine's personal account. Can you explain that?"

"No. Beth and I have no business dealings."

"Well we can prove that you have been blackmailing Beth Alewine for some time now," Grimes said. He then produced the sorority pictures showing Mary Ann and Beth in the Delta Zeta house. "Here's another of you two at a University of Georgia homecoming dance and yet another selling concessions at a football game. Care to revise your story?"

"Yes. I knew Beth. So what?"

"Did you know that she dated Ed Lawson and was pregnant with his child? Did you also know that she murdered the infant and dropped out of college?"

"I had nothing to do with any of that. Beth was on drugs. She went off the beam. I didn't know what happened to her until I moved to Rutherford, married Dennis, and got involved with community events."

"And when Beth decided to run for public office, you saw your opportunity to blackmail her about her pregnancy and the death of the infant. The present Ms. Alewine was not only straightened out, but she was a prominent attorney who had married into a wealthy family. When Beth decided to run for office, it was ka-ching. You knew she would pay any price to keep her past out of the media. You also knew about her alternate identity. For the right price, you'd keep quiet and have a nice little nest egg for the luxuries your penurious husband would not provide. But then Ed Lawson showed up and got himself killed. That put a serious kink in your plans, didn't it?"

Mary Ann's expression changed to anger. "Okay. You're right on the first part. I did blackmail Beth. She was a slut and deserved what she got, but I didn't kill Dennis. He was a bit of a tightwad, but I did love him in my own way."

At that point I was glad she couldn't see my face. I couldn't have come up with a character in my novels that was more cold-hearted. Mary Ann was a great actress. She certainly had me fooled and apparently she deceived a lot of others including Dennis.

Mary Ann continued, "Pamela came to town when Stephanie's books became so popular. I did a background check and made the connection that Ed was her brother. I saw an opportunity for her to avenge Ed's death. I tried to persuade Dennis to sell his formula for the anti-nausea medicine to one of the highest bidders. He wouldn't hear of it. We had a horrible quarrel and he walked out. I had no idea that he was going back to the lab that night. It was supposed to be off limits because of an earlier chemical spill. No one was to be in those buildings. Raymond, Pamela's loser husband, was going to break a few things, use a little pyrotechnics to start a small fire, and just give the college a scare. He wasn't supposed to blow up the damn place. The one thing I didn't bargain on was Pamela's lust for vengeance and Raymond's inept judgment."

"Then your testimony is that blowing up the laboratory and killing your husband was all Pamela's idea and you had nothing to do with it?" Grimes was going in for the kill.

"Absolutely. I understood Pamela's lust for avenging Ed's death, but the Alewines were in prison. What else was there to do about it? It was her idea to plant occultic symbols all over town in order to drag the Harts into the investigation. I was supposed to break into the Harts' home and toss stuff around to make it look like a robbery. That was supposed to lead the police off the trail. Pretty smart don't you think?"

Mary Ann looked pretty proud of herself. The woman I though worthy of being a supermodel wore a sneer which transformed her into an ugly vindictive bitch. The depths of my being couldn't conceive the hate she must feel for all of us. Yet she covered it so well.

Quinton, Harry, and I looked at each other in wonder. We couldn't believe all the stuff we were hearing. I couldn't wait to hear Pamela's side of the story.

18

As anxious as we were to hear more, I thought perhaps Uncle Harry had had enough excitement for one day. He and I picked up Khaki and headed to Harry's bungalow. I thought we both could use some of Harry's wine therapy.

I had a rough draft of the book I was writing in my tote, so I decided to make Uncle Harry a guinea pig. Perhaps it would get our minds off the present situation. The furor around Ed and our former relationship in college made my last book *Diva's Revenge* fly off the bookshelves. It was hard to think up a topic that would top revenge but I went back to the original *The Diva Code* and resurrected some characters. Part of that strategy was to persuade my readers who hadn't read the entire series to do just that. Also I got my protagonist into a lot of hot water, just like real life. Now I needed help to get her out of her predicament and right all the wrongs, without going over my word limit.

Harry said that he had read all of my books and guessed my identity before I publicly revealed it. I relied on his opinion of what my heroine would or would not do.

"Hell of a read," he said after going over the rough draft. "How does it end?"

"That's what I was hoping you could help me with," I said.

"I need a scotch, first. How about you?"

"What about your wine therapy?"

"Oh that's for pussies. Scotch is a man's drink."

"I'll have a Merlot," I said.

He tossed Khaki a treat on the way to the liquor cabinet. I took out a pen and prepared for corrections, suggestions, and ways to make this last book in the series the best yet. That's what any author worth his ink is always trying to do.

Quinton texted to say that Mary Ann was being booked for blackmail, but that's all she was confessing to. The critical thing would be if Pamela and her husband confessed to her part in Dennis' death.

He also said that after Harry's little tirade at the Java Station, Pamela hightailed it to who knows where so there's an APB out on her. I'd lay odds that Carol and Doris find her before the police. They left the Java Station right after she did supposedly to go home, but those women have taken this as their personal mission especially after learning about Khaki's poisoning.

I'm sure Doris has alerted the golden age community so if Pamela was in a 50-mile radius she would have been spotted by someone. If I were Pamela and two old biddies were trailing me, where would I lead them? And what would I do if I got them to follow me? The results make me quake.

The fact remains that Pamela DID poison Khaki, so that is grounds of arrest. But then I'm worried about my senior partners in crime on her tail. Maybe that wasn't such a good idea. I hope they stay hidden. A murder whether accidental or premeditated was committed at our back door. Lord knows even with their spy equipment, Carol and Doris are no match for a desperate woman like Pamela Jones. I kept this to myself. Harry was sipping Scotch and brushing Khaki. He seemed to have calmed himself.

"Quinton said he would be home late and for us not to wait dinner," I said.

"Oh don't worry about dinner for me. I ate a big lunch and with all the excitement it hasn't quite settled," Harry answered. He pulled a ball out of the cabinet and took Khaki into the back yard.

While Harry occupied himself, I phoned Doris. It went straight to voice mail. Then I phoned Carol. Same thing. My mind began racing with possibilities. I did the only thing I could think of.

"Detective Grimes. I believe my friends Carol and Doris are in danger."

My next call was to Quinton. His voice mail picked up.

"Harry has Khaki. I have to find Carol and Doris. I'll explain later. I love you."

"Uncle Harry. Could you babysit Khaki for a while? I have some things to do before dinner," I said.

"Sure. But when you return, we'll get back to the case, right?" Harry threw the ball to Khaki again. I'm not sure who was enjoying this the most.

"Of course," I lied.

19

I slid into my car. Quinton returned my call. I brought him up to speed on what had transpired.

"Pamela is still nowhere to be found," he said.

"That's what I was afraid of when she left the coffee shop in such a hurry. Pamela knows we are onto her. And what's more, I'm afraid that Carol and Doris are trailing her. They have no idea what she's capable of. I alerted Grimes but I don't know if he will take me seriously. So I have to take action."

"Action. What action? This isn't a novel. This is real life," Quinton replied.

"I took the precaution of putting a bug in Doris' tote bag for a time such as this. She's not the only one who has spyware."

"What are you saying?"

"I'm saying that Mary Ann and now Pamela have shown their true colors. Pamela drives a new white VW that's a rental."

Quinton snapped "And I'm saying that you and the girls are in danger. Where do you think Pamela would lead them if she realized she's being trailed?"

"Maybe the rec center. The seniors have a room for exercise, ballroom dancing, and yoga," I guessed.

"Really? Yoga and ballroom dancing?"

"Quinton, dear. Times have changed. Time to catch up with the modern seniors who take cruises in their golden years. Meet me at the senior center. Pronto."

I broke more than a few speed limits on my way to the center located in the Rutherford Convention Center. I breathed a sigh of relief when I spotted Doris' station wagon parked in a handicapped space. But the relief was only temporary when I saw a white VW convertible only a short distance away.

Quinton pulled in behind me. "Call the police," I shouted. "I have to find Carol and Doris."

He gave me a glare that spoke volumes, but I ignored it. My friends were in that building with a poisoner. Someone like that wouldn't blink at doing away with two old ladies.

I crept to the edge of the doorway leading to the exercise room. I heard Carol singing at the top of her lungs

Kumbaya my Lord, Kumbaya
Kumbaya my Lord, Kumbaya
Kumbaya my Lord, Kumbaya
Oh Lord, Kumbaya

Someone's praying Lord, Kumbaya
Someone's praying Lord, Kumbaya
Someone's praying Lord, Kumbaya
Oh Lord, Kumbaya

"Shut up woman or I'll shut you up," came a voice that I recognized as Pamela.

Then I heard Doris say, "Carol always sings when she's nervous. It's just a habit. She doesn't even realize that she does it."

Pamela raised her tone a level, "Shut her up or you'll both be sorry. I don't carry this for nothing."

That was my cue that Pamela not only had them corralled somehow but she was brandishing a weapon.

Someone's crying Lord, Kumbaya
Someone's crying Lord, Kumbaya
Someone's crying Lord, Kumbaya
Oh Lord, Kumbaya

There was Carol again. Bless her she was braver than I realized. My phone signaled a message from Doris.

"Help. Pamela has a gun."

I hid in the shadows as best I could. From my viewpoint, I saw that the girls' wrists were tied with what appeared to be electrical cords. Carol's voice wavered as she repeated the lyrics over and over. Sometimes she was louder, sometimes softer.

"Will you shut up?" Pamela yelled. "I can't think. Where is that good for nothing husband of mine? Raymond got us into this mess with his pyrotechnic crap. Now he's got to get us out of it. Mary Ann said it would be easy. Little did she know that my greedy husband would complicate things – big time."

Pamela dialed her phone again with apparently no answer since she slammed it back into her purse. Around the same time I saw a glint of light and what I thought was movement on the other side of the room. I was praying it was Grimes, the cavalry, or anyone but Raymond.

My eyes were gradually adjusting to the dim emergency lighting. Carol was still humming with Pamela shushing her in intervals. I heard the click of fingernails on a keyboard and surmised that Raymond had yet to answer. I prayed that he was trussed like a Thanksgiving turkey in one of the squad cars.

As if on cue, Carol suddenly stopped singing. She cleared her voice and began reciting:

Our Father which art in heaven,
Hallowed be thy name

Pamela's head swiveled around like it was on a spindle. She couldn't believe what was coming out of Carol's mouth. If I hadn't been in stealth mode, I would have chuckled.

Carol's hands were folded and in a more serene manner, she continued:

Thy kingdom come,
Thy will be done in earth, as it is in heaven
Give us this day our daily bread.

"This is the last time Doris. Shut her up!" Pamela demanded.

"I told you. When Carol gets nervous she does things, reciting scripture and singing are only two of them," Doris explained.

"I don't think you understand, dear. This is a hostage situation and YOU are the hostages. So keep quiet and do what I say," Pamela said.

And forgive us our debts,
as we forgive our debtors.
And lead us not into temptation,
but deliver us from evil:
For Thine is the kingdom, and the power,
and the glory, forever. Amen.

"Well, Thank God. That's over," Pamela said.

"Yes it is," a voice from the darkness agreed. "Hands up, Ms. Jones. You are under arrest for the murder of Dr. Dennis Camden, for poisoning an animal, and for being an accomplice to blackmail."

Pamela glared at me on her way out. Even wearing handcuffs, it was hard to believe my trusted agent was capable of such crimes.

I overheard her say that it was a relief to be rid of the singing and the chanting.

"Doris. Carol. Are you okay? Did Pamela hurt you?"

"No. We're fine," Doris said.

"Carol. You are a trooper. How did you come up with singing and chanting to rattle her nerves?" I asked.

"When my nephew puts on his music it drives me up the wall until he puts on his headphones, so I figured that a little Christian music wouldn't hurt the Madam," Carol said with confidence. "Besides I like singing and I recite the Lord's Prayer every day. It suddenly occurred to me that I hadn't done it today. No time like the present."

God's guardian angels were working overtime with those two. I hugged and kissed them both and guided them to the paramedics. I wanted to be sure they were okay. Quinton was outside with Detective Grimes who assured me that Raymond was subdued. He and Pamela were headed to the police station where charges would be filed.

Mary Ann sang like a bird when the district attorney offered to lighten her sentence if she could provide evidence that she was innocent of the explosion. Miss Pamela and Mr. Raymond will have a few choice phrases to say about her. For now I counted my blessings and collected my husband. It had been a long day.

We pulled into the driveway. Harry with Khaki on lead came to greet us. Both of them were happy as could be.

"Did you catch them? Damn. I wish I could have been there when they clamped on the handcuffs."

"Yes we got them. Pamela and MaryAnn plus their silent partner, Raymond, are on their way to jail." I walked him through the standoff at the senior center, replayed Carol's singing of *Kumbaya* and the final coup de grad of her recitation of the Lord's Prayer. He roared with laughter.

"I'm glad you got that bitch. Her husband was the one who blew up the lab?" Harry asked.

"Yes evidently he prided himself on being a pyrotechnical genius only he got this one wrong," I said.

"When the team finished examining the lab, he left clues here and there. He almost blew himself up in the process. Dennis wasn't supposed to be there. He surprised Raymond. They fought and Dennis hit his head. Raymond panicked and he blew up the lab and almost blew himself up along with it," Quinton added.

"I'm just glad this whole mess with the Alewines, the Camdens, and the Lawsons is over for good. Maybe now I can get back to writing, living my life, and dealing with murders only in print," I said as I poured a glass of red, kicked off my shoes, and pulled Khaki into my lap.

Sheila S. Hudson is the author of the Thursday Club series: *Murder at Golden Palms, Murder at Sea, Murder at the Mandelay, Murder at the Monastery, and Murder on the Marquee.* These are cozy mysteries all published by Take Me Away Books. Coming for the holidays: *Murder Under the Christmas Tree.*

She is also the author of two nonfiction books: *13 Decisions That Will Change Your Life* and *13 Decisions That Will Transform Your Marriage* (Dancing with Bear Publishing). Sheila has contributed to *Not Your Mother's Book* (2*), Chocolate for Women* (8), *Chicken Soup, Patchwork Path* (2*), Love Stories* (2) plus numerous periodicals.

Her byline also appears in Purple Pros and Costumer Magazine. Bright Ideas, the parent company, was established to bring hope and inspiration through the written/spoken word. Since 1983, Sheila has been affiliated with Southeastern Writers Association including two terms as president.   Contact her: sheilahudson.writer@gmail.com; www.13decisions.com or www.sheilahudsonwriter.com

Sheila and her husband, Timothy L. Hudson (shown in photo), have worked in campus ministry for over 30 years -- 5 years with Christian Student Fellowship at Northern Kentucky University and 28 years at Christian Campus Ministry at the University of Georgia. They have been married for 48 years and have two daughters, a son, and seven grandsons.

When she is not writing, you will find her knitting or making jewelry or plying small children with M&Ms.